Praise for *The Ghouls of Howlfair*

"Hilarious, spooky and full of unexpected twists! Molly Thompson is sharp, smart and persistent, and the perfect hero to lead us through this delightfully dark world."
Jenni Spangler, author of *The Vanishing Trick*

"This spooky mystery is brilliantly written, VERY funny and has the BEST female protagonist I have come across in an age — in fact, I would gladly follow Molly Thompson to the Gates of Hell and back! Utterly brilliant!"
Imogen White, author of the Rose Muddle Mysteries series

"A fabulously spooky read from the start. So refreshing to see a bold, resourceful and empathetic female protagonist who isn't afraid to stand out! I devoured this book in nearly one sitting. Nick has just made one heck of a splash onto the scene of spooky middle-grade fiction."
Lindsay Currie, author of *The Peculiar Incident on Shady Street*

"There are so many truly great and iconic girls of literature — Matilda and Pippi Longstocking, Jo March and Lyra Belacqua to name just a few. For me, the daringly determined Molly Thompson lives amongst these legends now, with no doubt that she'll become a timeless character of children's fiction."
Fern Tolley, Bluebird Reviews

"Ghoulish and creepy and deliciously funny. The characters are unforgettable, the dialogue is spot on and it's a cracking fast read."

MOLLY THOMPSON AND THE CRYPT OF THE BLUE MOON

NICK TOMLINSON

WALKER
BOOKS

First published 2020 by Walker Books Ltd
87 Vauxhall Walk, London SE11 5HJ

2 4 6 8 10 9 7 5 3 1

Text © 2020 Nick Tomlinson
Cover illustrations © 2020 Kim Geyer

The right of Nick Tomlinson to be identified as author
of this work has been asserted by him in accordance
with the Copyright, Designs and Patents Act 1988

This book has been typeset in Book Antiqua and Youbee

Printed and bound by CPI Group (UK) Ltd, Croydon CR0 4YY

British Library Cataloguing in Publication Data:
a catalogue record for this book is available from the British Library

ISBN 978-1-4063-8669-1

www.walker.co.uk

MIX
Paper from
responsible sources
FSC® C020471

For Jayne and my superb family,
with an extra high-five for my amazing sister Sarah,
and a big shout-out to the brilliant Evie Bee!

The Ghouls Are (Possibly) Back in Town

LATELY, THE THING THAT MOLLY THOMPSON worried about most, the noxious notion that kept her awake at night, the putrid possibility that stretched her small hours long, was the thought that the ghouls of Howlfair might be coming back.

Right now, though, Molly was more worried that she might be about to slam into a wall at forty miles per hour.

With a book (*Prophecies of Certain Doom*, by Yehudi Mantle) pressed to her stomach, the young amateur historian had only one free hand with which to cling to the rider of the bicycle that sped her, swift as a squandered Sunday, through the snoozy evening streets. Molly's teeth rattled as the cyclist pedalled recklessly over the uneven cobbles of Stayhand Walk.

"Felicity! Do we have to go so fast?" Molly's voice turned operatic as the bike juddered over the stones.

7

"Stop yodelling at me, Thompson!" called the cyclist. "I can't ride and listen to you at the same time."

"Felicity, mind that cat!"

A madcap swerve prevented a collision with a surprised-looking tabby, and caused Felicity Quick's dyed purple hair to fly into Molly's mouth. She spat it out.

"Sorry, cat!" Molly called over her shoulder.

Felicity tutted loudly. "I swear, if you apologize to one more cat, I'm gonna make *you* cycle."

Felicity steered the bike suddenly leftwards, across the cobbly road, and bunny-hopped it onto the far pavement.

Instinctively Molly clutched the plastic mask that was sitting on top of her head, to stop it flying off.

"Felicity, what are you doing?" Molly shouted into the rush of air.

At hurricane speed the bike plunged into the criss-cross of slender alleyways that led towards the memorial gardens and, further on, St Fell's Church. The bike chain whirred as the cycle freewheeled past the NO CYCLING sign.

"We're taking a short cut."

Autumn was upon them; the valley air had teeth. The cold wind was making Molly's eyes water.

"Too fast!"

Some of the painted wooden stalls had been put out in anticipation of tomorrow's Long Alley Dairy Market. At one point, only Felicity's fearless steering spared the girls from ending up shipwrecked on Mrs Bowman's Butter Wagon.

Felicity blew a raspberry. *"Get here pronto,* you said. *The ghouls are back, and we have to get Mr Wetherill,* you said..."

Wallace Wetherill was the only grown-up in Howlfair who'd believed Molly when, earlier that year, she'd claimed that the ghouls from one of her town's scariest legends were real and were killing people. Later, after Molly had cunningly trapped the ghouls in a crypt under Loonchance Manor on the night of the blue moon, Mr Wetherill had helped banish their demon-worshipping master, creepy local philanthropist Benton Furlock. And when the ghouls later vanished from the crypt, Mr Wetherill had bravely agreed to help track them down, even though he hadn't hunted monsters in Howlfair for over a decade.

Now Molly desperately needed the grumpy old monster-hunter's help. She'd found something in an obscure old book that had convinced her that the ghouls were definitely on the loose once more.

Felicity's father's locksmith bag, slung over her shoulder, clanked as the bicycle zigzagged between the stands.

"So here I am, being your personal chauffeur — again! — and suddenly you're all *Oh, Felicity, mind that cat! Oh, Felicity, you're going too fast! Oh, Felicity, maybe we should stop for a minute to admire the stars...*"

"I just don't want us to end up splattered against a wall so they have to clean us off the bricks with a flipping hosepipe!" Molly shouted as the bicycle bumped along. *"Look out!"*

The girls ducked under the lethally sharp wrought-iron sign that jutted from outside Gribley's Television Repair Shop.

"If I were you," Felicity shouted, "I'd be more worried about what your mum's gonna do to you when she finds out you've sneaked out of the house because you've had yet another mad notion that the ghouls are back!"

Molly flushed with dread. If Mum found out that Molly was disobeying her, she'd never trust her again. It would break their already fragile relationship in a way that Molly didn't think she'd be able to fix.

Down, down the bike plummeted — past the first of the two junctions that cut across Long Alley.

Then up, up the bike surged, past the second.

Flying over the junction, Molly glanced left, and for a brief, impossible moment, she thought she spotted the Grim Reaper drifting towards the northern entrance to the memorial garden, heading in the same direction as Felicity and Molly. Towards Mr Wetherill, who, she'd learned that evening, had been admitted to the infirmary.

"You've gone quiet," shouted Felicity. "Have you died?"

Molly opened her eyes. She let go of Felicity and pulled her plastic Dracula mask over her face to block out the blasting wind. Ahead, a mocking moon leered down at the vast basin of the Ethelhael Valley.

She said, simply, "Go faster."

Girls or Ghouls?

ELEVEN MINUTES BEFORE THE EXPLOSION IN Howlfair Infirmary, a nurse was doing the rounds. It was nearly ten o'clock and most of the patients in the Genevieve Wakeley Ward were asleep. One or two were half-dozing, nodding into books or magazines by the glow of their bedside lamps. Light from the corridor hazed through small windows and gave Mrs Marrable, in the end bed, a spectral radiance.

Moments after the nurse departed, Wallace Wetherill thought he heard his name being called from the enclosed garden at the back of the ward. The former werewolf-hunter sat up with a gasp. Fear played a minor-key glockenspiel solo on his spine. He'd been searching for a gang of missing ghouls for two months and had found nothing; but he'd often had the sensation, as he'd trudged around the lonely places of his town, of being secretly observed. Perhaps, tonight, the ghouls had decided to come for *him*.

Well, despite his injuries, he wasn't going to go down without a fight.

Fight? an old, familiar voice in his head sneered. *You're a coward, not a fighter. A lily-livered cur! A caitiff! A —*

The giant scarecrow-like man sighed and climbed out of bed. His joints wheezing like antique hydraulics. A cow-like snore from Mrs Marrable made Wallace Wetherill wobble.

See! You're spineless, Wallace. I've seen more backbone in a ripe banana.

"Well, this is one ripe banana who isn't going to be eaten by ghouls," he said gruffly.

"Huh?" said Elsie Turner in a nearby bed.

"Go back to sleep, Elsie," coughed Wetherill. "You're dreaming."

Shuffling painfully to the window, he reached inside his peach-coloured floral dressing gown and drew forth a pair of small antique muskets loaded with ghoul-fire pellets. He handled them carefully, reminding himself what would happen if he accidentally squeezed the triggers: half his fellow patients would be set ablaze in a screaming blast of sulphur; and, at the very least, the other half would be freed from the burden of eyebrows.

Wallace Wetherill didn't like guns. He'd never liked hunting werewolves. He was a quiet man who, in his spare time, enjoyed growing potatoes in the misty allotments near the cider orchards. He'd never actually killed a werewolf. He had once inconvenienced a badger. For the last ten years he'd devoted himself to running Wetherill's Weaponry Store, the horror-themed gift shop on Longmorrow Lane which sold plastic crossbows and stakes and crosses and fake silver bullets and local fudge. His muskets had slept in their walnut case, locked in the shop's safe — until earlier that summer, when a series of unbelievable events involving some local children had forced Wallace Wetherill back into the monster-hunting business.

As you know, the monster-hunting business is fraught with danger. Yesterday, for example, while searching the upper rooms of Loonchance Manor, Wallace put his foot in a metal paint kettle and fell down a staircase. Now he was in hospital with two cracked ribs and a fractured cheekbone and a black eye and a dramatic puffy bandage around his head. To be honest, his hopes of defending himself against a ghoul attack were slim, even with the monster-slaying muskets. His most realistic hope was that any ghoul attempting to bite his head off would choke on the bandage.

He squinted past his reflection, out at the crooked

trees and the statues and those odd stone markers that sprouted from the grass like raised cobbles. Fearfully he scanned the hawthorn bushes that hedged the garden in, and —

There it was again. "Mr Wetherill!"

A girl's voice.

"Don't be fooled, Wallace," Wetherill whispered to himself. "Ghouls can take any form."

That wasn't strictly true; ghouls can't take the form of a tree or a microwave oven. But they can shape-shift to impersonate humans, which is probably what Wallace meant.

"Mr Wetherill, over here, by the statue!"

Breathless, lung-locked, Wallace spotted two faces peeking out from either side of the statue of a lantern-bearing angel: a vampire face and a clown face.

"It's me, Mr Wetherill! Molly Thompson!"

The small ghoul calling itself Molly Thompson tiptoed forth into the pool of light spread by the angel's lantern. Then the ghoul/girl lifted its plastic Dracula mask to reveal a face very much like that of the meddlesome amateur historian: the frowning adamant eyes; the long straight nose; the little round mouth — all framed by scribbles of brown hair that curled up stubbornly at the ends, determined not to fall.

"You don't fool me, shapeshifter!" Wetherill growled

under his breath. He noticed that his muskets were wobbling in his hands. "No time for cowardice, Wallace. If that fiend takes one more step, smash the window and blast it back to Hell!"

The Molly-shaped ghoul/girl moved towards the infirmary —

Wetherill lurched forward to break the glass with the butt of a musket —

Then the ghoul/girl tripped over one of the decorative cobbles, and fell on its face.

It lifted its head, and Wetherill saw on the creature's face an expression he'd seen before. Twice before, in fact.

He'd seen it on the face of the *real* Molly Thompson, in his shop on Longmorrow Lane, back when she'd been the first person in town to stand up to him. (He was known for being something of an ogre.)

And he'd seen the same Molly Thompson wear an identical expression when she'd emerged, battered and hopping, from Loonchance Manor, having returned to a ghoul-filled vault to rescue a boy named Carl Grobman — the boy who'd lured her there in the first place.

Wallace realized that the thing approaching him was not a ghoul. No ghoul could mimic that look of serious, maddeningly stubborn determination.

He lowered his hands. "Molly."

In Walks Death

MOLLY LAY ON THE GRASS OUTSIDE THE infirmary. Over her shoulder she saw Felicity Quick breaking cover and rushing, clown-masked, towards her. Not long ago — before Felicity had saved Molly's life beneath Loonchance Manor — the sight of the athletic bully rushing towards her would have meant only one thing to Molly: an enthusiastic beating. But Felicity Quick extended a hand and hoisted Molly to her feet, and the girls made their way towards the ward.

At the window, Felicity unzipped her dad's locksmith bag and set about trying to prise the window open.

"What do you think you're doing?" Wetherill hissed, checking over his shoulders to see if anyone in the ward was still awake. "Molly Thompson, you promised your mother on your life that you'd never sneak out of the guest house again."

"I know," Molly said through the glass. "But I think I've found out what's happened to our ghouls. I think they're on the loose, and I wanted to tell you as soon as possible so we can come up with a plan. But it's after visiting hours so Felicity borrowed her dad's locksmith tools so we could break in and speak to you."

"Why are you wearing masks?"

"So nobody recognizes us," sighed Felicity. "Obviously." The window frame emitted a sharp *crack!* Wallace winced.

"Will you stop ruining that window frame!"

Wedging the muskets between his knees, Mr Wetherill fumbled with the latch and opened the window from the inside. The girls dodged as it swung wide.

"Mrs Mayhew saw you being put in an ambulance near Loonchance Manor last night," Molly whispered through the open window. She could hear a chorus of snores behind Mr Wetherill. "She told Felicity's gran, who told Felicity's granddad this evening, and Felicity overheard the conversation when she was on the toilet…"

"Too much detail," said Felicity.

"Sorry. Anyway, Felicity called me, and then I phoned Lowry" — Lowry was Molly's best friend — "and she's sneaked off to let herself into her dad's office and steal some keys to the Kroglin Mausoleum so we can have an emergency meeting, and —"

"Wait — Lowry Evans is breaking into the tourist office?"

"Well, no, she's pinched her dad's keys, so technically she's just trespassing."

Suddenly there came a scream from the other side of the ward. Mrs Marrable was kneeling on her bed in the corner of the ward, peering through the window into the lit white corridor beyond.

"It's Death! The Grim Reaper!" she cried. "He's come for someone!" She scrambled like a puppy, entangling herself in her duvet. "Nigel, I think he's come for you!"

Nigel fell out of bed and blundered towards the corridor window to look. Molly could just make out the dark shape moving in the passageway beyond. She remembered seeing a hooded figure in town earlier, hefting a scythe...

"But it's not my time!" Nigel yelped, giving Mrs Marrable a shake.

"Oh, he's coming!" sobbed Mrs Marrable, flinging Nigel aside and back-peddling until she tripped over the notoriously large feet of Elsie Turner, who was trying to hide under her bed.

"Everyone get behind me!" shouted Wallace

19

Wetherill, and Molly watched open-mouthed as the giant man took position in the centre of the ward. But the other patients didn't notice him. They were too busy wailing and trying to hide behind each other, or falling out of beds, or swimming helplessly across the floor.

Then the door swung open and in walked Death, scythe in hand.

The Grim Reaper was much shorter than anyone had expected him to be. Also, he was wearing orange glittery trainers.

"Lowry," Molly gasped, as Mr Wetherill fired both muskets at her best friend.

Tomorrow's News

THE MUSKETS MADE A SOUND LIKE TWO very large bubble-gum bubbles popping, and green smoke engulfed Mr Wetherill's head. The guns must have become very hot all of a sudden, because Wetherill yelped and threw them under a bed — empty, thankfully — to his left, at which point both guns, belatedly, went off.

Molly watched horrified as a blinding claw of green fire wrapped around the bed and gave it a squeeze. Within seconds the bed was a charred frame. Swamp-coloured smoke, smelling of brimstone and kippers, billowed across the ward. The patients choked and wailed. Felicity shouted "Cripes!" and staggered away from the window — but Molly remained, gripping the sill, searching desperately for her friend.

Screaming shapes twisted and dashed in the smoky darkness.

A door opened — a nurse had arrived and was shouting for backup. "Lowry!" Molly cried, but her words were lost in the hubbub.

Now Mr Oberman had sprained an ankle trying to flee, and had collapsed in front of the doorway, blocking the escape route, so most patients had decided to either hide or flail aimlessly around the ward. More staff members arrived and began trying to shoulder the door open, not knowing that Mr Oberman was groaning on the other side. Mr Frodsham blasted Mrs Marrable with a fire extinguisher. The thick smoke had gone blue and now smelled of cardamom and socks. Suddenly a nimble shape emerged from the smoke and laid a skeletal hand upon Mr Wetherill's shoulder. He screamed. It was Lowry Evans, still with her hood up.

"Hi, Mr Wetherill," Lowry said brightly from beneath her hood, while the smoke turned red behind her and began to smell like cinnamon and wet dogs, and the screaming intensified, and Mrs Marrable began attacking people at random with a walking frame. "Rather lively in here, isn't it?"

Wetherill gnashed his teeth. "Lowry Evans, get through that window before I shove this bandage down your throat."

"Right-o, Mr W," said Lowry, while six patients

struggled to pull Mr Oberman from the doorway. "Oh, hi, Molly. Grab my scythe, will you?"

Death crawled out of Howlfair Infirmary, face first, and flopped ungracefully onto the grass outside.

Molly looked at Wallace's stricken expression as the smoke turned yellow behind him. "I'm sorry, Mr Wetherill. We just thought — "

"Listen, Molly Thompson," Wallace growled as Lowry got to her feet and dusted herself down. "I've been searching for your ruddy missing ghouls for months now, and the only ghouls I've seen are the stupid knitted toy ones they've put in Loonchance Manor to make the place more family-friendly for its grand reopening."

"Oh, I've seen the notice board!" said Lowry. "'*The Loonchance Manor Fun 'n' Frights Fantasia! Come and meet Gilbert the Ghoul and his gang of pathetic knitted sock puppet friends!*'"

"The reason I'm in here," Wetherill went on, clearing his throat and blushing a little, "is that I stepped in a paint kettle in Loonchance Manor and fell down some stairs looking for your blinking missing ghouls. And now you turn up to tell me some fresh nonsense about the ghouls coming back."

"It's not nonsense, Mr Wetherill," Molly said firmly.

"Not this time." Molly held up her dusty book. "This time I've got proof."

Mr Wetherill let out a sigh that could defrost a lorry's windscreen, and put a hand to his injured head. He turned to Lowry. "So you've got the keys to the Kroglin Mausoleum?"

Lowry saluted.

"Meet me there in ten minutes," Wetherill said to Molly. He looked with trepidation over his shoulder at the pitched pillow fight now taking place between two armies of patients hiding behind upturned beds. The indistinct shapes of Edna Marrable and Elsie Turner grappled in the gloom. "I'm not going to fit through that window — so I'm going to have to fight my way out of here." He turned a fearsome glare at Molly. "This proof of yours best be good, or I'm dragging you back to your poor mother and turning you in. And if she's sensible she'll ground you till you're twenty."

And with that, he waded wearily into the smoke.

"Kroglin Mausoleum had better be soundproof," grumbled Felicity, leading the way back through the garden. "I need to scream at Lowry."

"Scream at me for what, exactly?" Lowry said, indignant, trying to keep up with Felicity. Dramatically she threw back her hood to reveal a charming elfin

24

face and a very un-Death-like bob of golden hair.

"What do you think?" Felicity hissed, gesturing back towards the now-empty ward with the blackened bed. "For turning tonight's perfectly simple rescue mission into tomorrow's front-page news."

Kroglin Mausoleum

THE GIRLS PRESSED EASTWARD THROUGH Howlfair, past silent shops aglow with street-lamp light. They went along one of the three long roads that formed a triangle known as the Circuit, up past the Dance Square with its bandstand. The huge hanging bell nicknamed Old Mercy. The horrible street lamps made of bone.

"Molly, you're shivering," Felicity tutted. "Why didn't you bring a coat?" She sounded annoyed rather than concerned.

"It's in the wash," mumbled Molly. "I leaned against a wall that my mum had just painted."

"What, you've only got one coat?"

Molly blushed and said nothing.

Felicity turned to Lowry. "What on earth possessed you to turn up at a hospital ward disguised as the Grim Reaper?" she snapped. "Also, we agreed to meet outside, by the window, and instead you saunter through the ward swinging a scythe around. How did you even get past the reception desk?"

"Silent are the tiny feet of Death," said Lowry in a haunted chant. "Also, Larry on reception had his hand trapped in the drinks machine again, so I just strolled past him."

"I swear, Lowry Evans, next time we —"

"Next time we what? Next time Molly Thompson persuades us to break into a hospital so she can tell some clumsy old man her latest barmy speculations about some missing ghouls right after he's had an accident looking for some missing ghouls?"

Molly said, "He's not a clumsy old man!"

"Are we talking about the same Mr Wetherill?" Lowry said. "The one who — just last month — got his trousers caught in a taxi door outside the cinema where they were showing *Gone With the Wind*?" She gave a shudder and followed Felicity over a broken fence. "I still have nightmares about those beige Y-fronts."

"Oh, and let's not forget the time he nearly shot Lowry's head off with weird muskets that fired magical fireballs of death," added Felicity.

"I remember it like it was yesterday," sighed Lowry. "Or, more accurately, sixteen and a half minutes ago."

"OK, so he's getting a bit accident-prone," said Molly as the girls negotiated the scrubby fields beyond the town hall, heading to where Kroglin Mausoleum glared out from within a secretive council of oaks. "But we need Mr Wetherill's help right now. I'll explain everything at the mausoleum. But basically I've discovered that we're in a lot of danger."

"You're the one who's in danger, Molly," Lowry piped up. "Your guesthouse is falling apart and all the guests are leaving, your poor mother is stressed out of her mind, and you promised her you'd never sneak out at night again, and when she finds out you've disobeyed her to rescue some old guy who stepped in a bucket, she'll have a meltdown that'd make the vilest ghoul in Hades look like Flopsy the Sock Puppet."

The children passed through the copse. Recently, Howlfair Tourist Board had been working to turn Kroglin Mausoleum into a Werewolf Museum. (Lowry's dad worked for the tourist board, and she'd pinched the key from his office.) There was a sign by the fence:

> OPENING THIS HALLOWE'EN!
> THE KROGLIN MAUSOLEUM
> WEREWOLF MUSEUM
> An interactive history of lycanthropy in
> Howlfair.
> Enjoy games, displays, cream teas,
> eyebrow-threading!
> Meanwhile, beneath your feet, in the
> VAST CRYPTS below, the remains of the
> doomed Kroglin family — suspected of
> harbouring werewolves and murdered by
> a mob — rest in peace...
> OR DO THEY????

"That sign doesn't make sense," said Lowry. "And look at that picture of a werewolf! It looks like a badger with a perm. Words cannot describe how rubbish it is. In fact, I need to make up a word to describe how rubbish it is." She pondered. "My word is 'wobbish'."

An irritable wind pierced the ring of trees and wound itself protectively around the mausoleum. The girls pushed through it to the big iron front door, which was embossed with wolves. Most of the wolves had been dented by mallets swung centuries ago by the same angry townsfolk who'd murdered the Kroglin family. Above the door, on a shield, was the Kroglin family crest: an hourglass through which tiny stars trickled, with a sleeping wolf beneath it.

Lowry had said she'd chosen this place to smuggle Mr Wetherill because it was close to the infirmary (it wasn't) and because Mr Wetherill would be comfortable here (he wouldn't). Molly knew the real reason: Lowry wanted to see inside the mausoleum before the place officially opened to the public. Lowry's pet theory was that her family was somehow connected to the Kroglin clan; she was terrified that she'd inherited the ancient werewolf curse of the House of Kroglin, and would suddenly become a lycanthrope one full moon.

A furious posse of townsfolk had almost completely demolished Kroglin Manor in 1711, leaving only the domed entrance hall intact, and this square stone edifice formed the basis of Kroglin Mausoleum. Underneath were the silent crypts. The stone wolves that once had capered along the roof's ledges were now shattered and headless. But the superb silver wolf at the top of the dome, its front paws raking at the sky, its fangy mouth mid-gnash, proudly remained, having been restored to gleaming glory by a mayor of Howlfair in the 1800s.

Lowry slammed the door, shutting out the wind. Inside the main hall, the girls found evidence of renovation. Paint-splattered sheets lay spread over the mosaic floor. There was scaffolding against one of the walls. Lunar luminescence filtered through the pearlescent dome overhead, which was decorated with silver embossed figures of wolves. Doors around the main hall led to other chambers. A huge wooden circular trapdoor in the middle of the main hall led underground to the vaults where the Kroglins, murdered, mouldered.

Molly examined the trapdoor, tracing the beam of her beloved Shadeshifter Tactical Flashlight around its circumference, eyeing the fizzy alien-seeming moss that sprouted from the wrought-iron edging and the bolts. She entertained a brief horrid image of the Kroglins' corpses in the crypts below covered in the same moss, and switched off her torch, spooked. There was a circular window hatch in the middle of the trapdoor. Molly put her hand to its heavy iron ring, then decided against opening it.

"It's colder than a snowball sandwich in here," Felicity grumbled. "We shouldn't be making Wetherill trudge over here when he's just injured himself looking for ghouls that've either gone back to Hell or are hiding somewhere waiting to be allowed back into Hell."

"I told you — the ghouls are on the loose," Molly said. "I've got proof."

"To be fair, Molly," said Lowry, "this is like the fifth time this month that you've told us you've got proof that the ghouls are back. And every time it turns out that you made some silly mistake. Which is weird, because Molly Thompson never makes silly mistakes."

"And even if you're right this time," said Felicity, "we shouldn't be expecting Wetherill to protect us. He's getting old."

"He's still strong," Molly objected. "Not too long ago I saw him pick up two shoplifters with one hand and throw them onto the street by their hair."

"Once I saw him sneeze the head off one of his shop's mannequins," said Lowry. "Not sure if that's relevant to our discussion."

Suddenly a whoosh of wind-song tugged the girls' attention to the mausoleum's door — it had swung grandly open and there, in a greatcoat, one hand pressed to his injured ribs, stood Wallace Wetherill.

Wendell Zoet

"I DON'T THINK ANYBODY IN THE INFIRMARY saw me fire the guns," Wetherill wheezed as he lumbered across the hall, his boots making echoes, the door swinging shut behind him. He took in the mausoleum as he walked. The dome that caught the hazy cloud-coddled moonlight. The circular trapdoor. "They were too busy looking at the ruddy Grim Reaper. But nevertheless there'll be an investigation into the infirmary explosion, and I'd rather not be around to face questioning. So I'll be disappearing for a while."

"But where will you go?" Molly asked.

"Somewhere secret, where I can get a few days' peace and quiet before I have to quell this ghoul invasion you claim is coming," he said, halting in front of her. "You've got two minutes, Molly Thompson. Show me your proof."

Hurriedly Molly scooped up her copy of *Prophecies*

of Certain Doom by Yehudi Mantle and got to her feet.

"Right there," said Molly, pointing at a picture.

"An old woodcut of Wendell Zoet," mumbled Wetherill.

"Who's Wendell Zoet?" asked Felicity.

"A soothsayer," said Molly, handing over the book. "He predicted —"

"He predicted something that would happen just before the Dark Days eventually came back," said Wetherill, studying the book. "About ten years after the people of Howlfair managed to drive away the town's monsters ..."

"So we're talking around 1744," Molly butted in.

"... Zoet said he looked into a crystal ball and saw something unspeakable..."

Lowry gasped. *"My sister."*

Molly ignored her. "He said that the evil things lurking in the valley would one day get summoned from their hiding places..."

"Sorry, but can perhaps just one of you speak?" Felicity said. "It's like watching a tennis match."

Molly blushed. "The thing is, in his crystal ball, Wendell Zoet saw a vision of a person, apparently a girl or a woman, leading someone — a boy or a man — through a crypt. And in his vision, these two people set something free."

"The evil that they released called forth from hiding everything in the valley that was similarly evil," concluded Wetherill. "In other words — the Dark Days returned to Howlfair. So…"

Molly said, "So the Mayor of Howlfair banned people from going into crypts in pairs, and the Dark Days didn't come back."

"End of story," said Wetherill, offering Molly her book back.

Molly didn't take it.

"Not quite," she said. "Howlfair's prophecies always come true — sooner or later. And I think this one has already started."

Keep Away from
Midnight Crypts

MOLLY REACHED INTO HER BACK POCKET
and drew out a small magnifying glass and
handed it to Mr Wetherill.

"At the bottom of the page, you can see Wendell
Zoet's actual prediction."

"I can't see it," Wetherill grumbled.

"Look through the glass. The book's old and faded,
but underneath the picture, there's an inscription."

"I only see squiggles."

"They're not squiggles, Mr Wetherill. The caption
is written in —"

"Odinic-Hermetic-Enochian hieroglyphs," Wetherill
muttered. "A mixture of magical symbols. Rare."

"But decipherable," said Molly, "if you know your
stuff."

Felicity tutted. "You two are proper geeks."

Molly gave Wetherill a dark glare. "It says *When*

the girl leads the boy from the crypt on the blue moon at midnight, the monsters therein will quit their slumber, and will summon all those as hellish as they, till the Dark Days return."

Wetherill lowered the magnifying glass and squinted at Molly.

"Don't you see, Mr Wetherill?" Molly said. "Two months ago I rescued Carl from the crypt under Loonchance Manor on the night of the blue moon! *I was the girl who led the boy from the crypt!* And it was around midnight! I made the monsters in the crypt — the ghouls — quit their slumber — so I triggered the prophecy! Now the ghouls will be summoning everything else as hellish as they are!"

"Oh God!" wailed Lowry. "My best friend brought back the Dark Days! My mum will never let me hear the end of this."

Wetherill rubbed a mutton-chop sideburn thoughtfully and handed back the book with a sigh.

"Aren't you going to say anything, Mr Wetherill?" Molly asked.

Eventually the old werewolf-hunter spoke. "I give you a B minus."

"Beg your pardon?"

"It's a good effort, Molly. But like the last seven times you've tried to convince me that the ghouls are back, you've made some silly mistakes."

Molly frowned. "Mistakes? Like what?"

"You need to brush up on your magical hiero-glyphs, Miss Thompson," Wetherill sighed. "For a start, this doesn't say that a girl — or woman — will lead a boy — or man — *from* a crypt. It says she'll lead him *into* a crypt. And you definitely didn't lead Carl Grobman into a crypt, did you? If I remember rightly, *he* led *you*."

"Molly doesn't like to talk about that," said Lowry. "She's still a bit angry that the weirdest kid in school tried to sacrifice her to a demon."

"Furthermore," Wetherill went on, "these glyphs don't say that monsters will be loosed in a crypt *on* the blue moon. It says the Crypt *of* the Blue Moon. See for yourself — the tiny symbol of an ibis indicates that it's a name, the name of an actual crypt."

Molly took back the magnifying glass and squinted at the page. Her heart jolted. Wallace was right.

"So where's this Crypt of the Blue Moon?" Felicity asked.

"It could be one of ten thousand crypts in Howlfair — we have more per acre than anywhere on earth," said Wetherill. "But the Crypt of the Blue Moon definitely isn't the crypt you found yourself in underneath Loonchance Manor, Molly."

"Why not?"

38

"Because you missed one last detail," said Wetherill. "These hieroglyphs don't say that *monsters* will be wakened. They say that *a monster* — singular — will be wakened, and it will summon all those as hellish as *itself*. And the glyph used for *monster* is referring to a specific kind of monster. Something dead — or, perhaps, *undead*."

"Like a phantom," Molly whispered, scratching her nose. "Or a vampire, or a zombie, or a putrimus..."

"Yes," said Wetherill. "But not a ghoul. Because ghouls —"

"Ghouls aren't dead," said Lowry. "Or undead. A ghoul is, um —" She looked at Molly. "It's a kind of egrimus. An evil spirit that can turn solid."

"Very good," said Wetherill.

"So — the ghouls aren't coming back?" said Lowry.

"Not that I know of," said Mr Wetherill. "Just stay away from crypts at midnight and you'll be fine. And if you must go into a crypt at midnight, don't lead any boys there..."

"Or men," said Lowry.

"Or men. And don't release anything dead or undead. Follow that advice, Molly Thompson, and I promise you won't trigger any ancient prophecies."

Molly turned the book over in her hands and stared at the floor. She didn't know whether to feel relieved or humiliated. She felt a bit of both.

"Mr Wetherill, are you going to drag me to my mum and turn me in?" she asked.

"No, I'm not going to turn you in," said Wetherill. "But listen, Molly. I can understand that you're frightened. You're scared that those ghouls you outwitted will come back for us. But the ghouls have gone — probably back to Hell — and this fear of yours seems to be clouding your brain."

"My brain isn't cloudy, thank you very much!"

Mr Wetherill pointed at Molly's book. "The Molly Thompson who bamboozled ghouls under Loonchance Manor wouldn't have made a string of silly mistakes reading Odinic-Hermetic-Enochian hieroglyphs," he said. "And she wouldn't have made any of the other silly mistakes you've been making recently."

"I reckon Molly secretly *wants* the Dark Days to come back," Felicity muttered.

Molly gasped, outraged.

"I'll make you a deal," Wetherill told Molly. "I won't report you to your mother. But this has to be the last time you contact me with a half-spun theory. The ghouls of Howlfair have moved on. It's time we moved on, too. I want you to do me a favour."

The glint in Wetherill's eye made Molly feel apprehensive. "What kind of favour?" Molly asked.

"Pay Carl a visit in the shop and tell him I'll be back

soon," Mr Wetherill said. "Make sure he's got enough food and tea bags. He's a resourceful lad, but I don't like to think of him alone all through the holidays."

Molly felt heat rise in her cheeks. Carl Grobman was a shifty loner in her class at school. An orphan who now lived in a room above Mr Wetherill's shop on Longmorrow Lane, he'd previously lived in the orphanage run by local ghoul-summoner Benton Furlock. Brainwashed by Furlock, he'd led Molly to think he was her friend, and helped Furlock lure her into a deadly trap in the cellars beneath Loonchance Manor. But Molly had escaped, and although Carl had apologized many times afterwards, she knew she could never trust him again. They had hardly spoken since.

"I'm sure we'll see him after half-term," Molly mumbled. "Back at school."

"Don't hate Carl, Molly," Wetherill said. "When you hate, you don't think straight." He shook his head and sighed. "I didn't mean for that to rhyme."

Molly scowled at the thought of seeing Carl. Lowry gave her a hearty slap on the back that made her eyes goggle. "Don't worry, Mr Wetherill," said Lowry, "we'll call round and check in on Carl tomorrow."

"Good. Now if you don't mind, I have to ask a friend if I can stay a few nights. Stay away from crypts at midnight, Molly Thompson — that's my advice."

The girls watched Wetherill tramp painfully away. At the doorway he raised a hand to bid them farewell, and launched himself into the windy night.

"Well, I for one have had a most enjoyable evening scaring people in hospital," sighed Lowry, putting her hood up. "And you must agree, Molly, that it's a relief to find out that, yet again, your suspicions about ghouls are a load of..."

"Wobbish," said Felicity.

"Exactly!" said Lowry, clapping. "A load of old wobbish. The ghouls aren't coming back, and the only thing we have to fear is your terrifying mother."

Molly turned the book over in her hands. "I'm sorry," she mumbled. "I don't know how I could have got the hieroglyphs wrong. I never get that sort of thing wrong."

"Maybe you just need a break from solving ancient puzzles and investigating terrifying mysteries and worrying yourself sick about nowhere-to-be-found ghouls," said Lowry, taking Molly's arm and leading her towards the door, Felicity following. "Concentrate on other stuff for awhile."

"Yeah," said Felicity, "like sneaking back into the Excelsior Guesthouse without your mother catching you and chopping your head off."

"Precisely," said Lowry.

The Excelsior Guesthouse

IF YOU WERE EVER TO WALK DOWN CECILY Craven Street, in the part of Howlfair known as the Guesthouse District, you'd be forgiven for finding yourself thinking about funerals.

It was a grave, vigil-silent road, broad enough for a hearse and mourners, with wreaths often left hanging in windows on account of some old obscure tradition. (Howlfair had lots of obscure traditions.) Stately, studded with imposing but infrequent black cast-iron street lamps, the road swept you down into the lush, tree-shaded basin of the Ethelhael Valley, proceeding through melancholy little parks with yew trees and commemorative statues that conjured thoughts of death, till at last Cecily Craven Street ended its journey, like the eighteenth-century music hall star Cecily Craven had ended hers, at Howlfair New Cemetery.

Most of the town's guesthouses were located on Cecily Craven Street, for historical reasons that most locals had forgotten. Molly, though, could give you the whole story of Howlfair's Guesthouse District if you asked her. She knew every inn and guesthouse along this road. They were what her mum called *the competition*. For Molly lived in one such guesthouse, at the bottom of Cecily Craven Street, the teetering tall one with the circular forecourt in front of it and Howlfair New Cemetery behind it. The Excelsior Guesthouse.

"Reckon you can sneak back in without getting caught?" Felicity asked Molly as she halted the bike near the hedgerows opposite the forecourt.

"There won't be anyone around to catch me," Molly said. "They are only five people staying at the guesthouse, and all of them are a hundred years old." She swung herself from the bike. "The front door gets locked at ten, but everyone's tucked up in bed by eight."

"What about your mum?"

"She'll still be up — but she'll probably be in the kitchen rewriting this week's menus," said Molly. "I accidentally forgot to put the meat delivery in the fridges, so the next seven days are Vegetarian Week."

Felicity squinted at the looming guesthouse, all

orange stone and black timber. "What would your mum do if she found out you'd run off without telling her?"

The thought made Molly's innards flutter. "We've been getting on really well lately. It's the first time we've been getting along in years — since..." Molly bit a nail.

"Since your dad died?"

"Yeah," said Molly. She became aware of the small vortex of sadness that was always rotating in her. She made the effort to shift her focus; she knew from experience that if she paid it any attention, it would get stronger and start to pull her into itself. "Even though she's really stressed about money and the guesthouse, she's managing to keep it together, and I know it's because we're not fighting anymore. She hasn't asked me anything else about what happened in the summer. She just made me promise to never sneak off again. Everything would be ruined if she found out I'd broken my promise."

"My parents won't even have noticed I'm gone," said Felicity, exaggerating a yawn. "Since Granddad had his heart attack they've been too busy fussing over him to pay me any attention. Which is fine by me, but it's driving Granddad doolally." She slapped Molly's shoulder. "I'll call for you tomorrow morning so we can check in on Grobman. In the meantime, try to have just one night where you don't lie awake fretting about ghouls."

Felicity rode off. Molly crunched across the gravel towards the guesthouse.

The jutting gable made it look like a ghost ship emerging from the cloud-webbed night. The crescent moon sat on one of the chimneys like a lookout in a crow's nest.

It was customary for the front door of the Excelsior to be locked by ten. But as Molly quietly fitted her key into the keyhole, she accidentally leaned on the handle and — *click!* — the door creaked open. The lamplit white lobby, snoozing to the rising ticks and falling tocks of a grandmother clock, appeared before her.

Why was the door unlocked?

Bell-Ringer

MOLLY SCANNED THE LOBBY: THE TABLE bearing the guestbook and the fancy white and gold telephone; the rows of pamphlets advertising spooky attractions; the wooden staircase, dreamily spiralling up to the first floor. The reception hatch was shut, as was the door to Mum's office.

To her left, beyond the clock, before the stairs, the door to the lounge was open. Vague light filtered through.

Tick? Tock. Tick? Tock. The grandmother clock asked and answered its eternal question. Then, just when Molly had decided that she was alone —

What was that noise?

Molly spun round. Too fast. Her leg buckled. She reached out to grab the bannister, but missed and fell. As she lay winded on the floor she heard the scuffling of feet somewhere in the darkness of the lounge...

Then came a muted clanking that Molly couldn't identify, followed by the pompous cackle of nosy Mr Banderfrith, her least-favourite resident.

"Ha!" Banderfrith barked triumphantly. "Molly Thompson, is that you?"

Molly scrambled into the dark space behind the spiral staircase.

"Sneaked out, did you? After promising your mother that you'd be in your bedroom all evening, working on your holiday assignment for school! Ha!"

Banderfrith pattered through the door and crossed the lobby tiles in his gingham slippers, walking stick thudding. He paused at the pool of light by the green-shaded lamp, squinting at the staircase. Molly squirmed backwards, deeper into the shadows.

"I made a promise to your mother too, Molly," Banderfrith went on. "I promised I would report any acts of daughterly disobedience I happened to catch you perpetrating."

Molly watched from the darkness as Mr Banderfrith, tufty moustache dancing upon his eager face, moved towards Molly.

She saw something in his free hand — something shiny...

"Under the stairs, eh, Molly? I can see the glint

of those beady eyes." He advanced. "Come forth, recalcitrant brat! You're cornered!"

Suddenly — of course! — Molly recognized the object in Banderfrith's hand. It was the large brass bell he rang to alert Mum to Molly's misdoings. He held the bell aloft, ready to wake everyone in the building.

"I will count," said Banderfrith darkly, "to three."

There was nowhere for Molly to go.

"One."

Her mind fizzled with excuses she could give her mother, excuses as to why Mr Banderfrith had caught her in the lobby of the Excelsior when she said she'd be in her room all evening ...

"Two."

... sneaking indoors with a vampire mask stuffed inside the hood of her sweatshirt...

"Three!"

Too late.

A Wig and a Prayer

WITH A BACKSWING BANDERFRITH SET THE
bell ringing. But its clangs were cut short — for
without warning, from the darkness of the lounge,
a set of fangs and amber eyes flew, and something
unspeakable leapt at the old man!

O ye gods — a ghoul!

A tiny ghoul eating Banderfrith alive! A frazzled
little shadow wearing a collar! Way too small to be a
ghoul, actually — but possibly an imp! And not exactly
eating Banderfrith alive, just hanging by its teeth from
his blazer sleeve, and —

It was, Molly realized, not a ghoul or an imp but
her pet cat, her companion throughout a thousand-
and-one adventures, a scraggly thing with very
few of his nine lives left. He'd shown up, as he had
so many times before, to rescue her from a sticky
situation.

"Gabriel!" Molly mouthed.

Banderfrith yowled and flung both beast and bell aside (the bell gave a surprised *klung!*), and spun to face his foe.

"Blasted cat!"

He lifted his walking stick like a golf club, and swung.

Gabriel rolled away but was clipped nonetheless, and Banderfrith gave chase.

"You're lucky I haven't got my sword-stick!" he spat, referencing his favourite cane, which (he claimed) concealed a deadly sharp fencing foil inside the hollowed-out middle. "Stop cowering, thou craven caitiff, and fight like a man!"

The cat dodged as the stick swooshed and Banderfrith leaped. With a gnash of anger, forgetting the importance of remaining hidden, Molly began to crawl like a commando from her hiding place to intervene. In the meantime, as Banderfrith lurched into a fencing lunge, another furry creature flew through the air and landed on the floor.

It was, Molly registered, Banderfrith's famously awful shiny black wig. Molly watched as Banderfrith and Gabriel paused to contemplate the fallen toupée.

Man and beast looked up and glared at each other. Then both raced to claim the hair.

Gabriel was quicker. Scooping up the wig in his jaws (Molly involuntarily coughed "Yuck!"), he dashed into the darkness of the lounge. Swinging his stick, sobbing with fury, Banderfrith pursued.

"Thief! Thief!"

Next came the inevitable response from upstairs: Mrs Hellastroom, who'd recently upgraded to a bigger room on the first floor, started shouting at Banderfrith to shut up. It was only a matter of time before Molly's mum arrived on the scene, summoned by the commotion.

Molly needed to get to her bedroom fast.

Molly stumbled up the first flight of stairs and could hear her mother directly overhead. She headed right, down the lamp-lit white corridor with its crooked black beams and the porthole windows in the doors. Looking for a hiding spot.

She tried a broom cupboard. Locked.

She tried the doors to bedrooms she knew were empty. (Most of them were empty.)

Locked.

Another door, and another: locked, locked. The footfalls reached the staircase. Not knowing what else to do, Molly sank to the carpet and lay down flat. She watched fearfully as the door to the stairwell sprang open and a horizontal whoosh of rose-gold hair surged by like an intercity express —

— straight past her!

Molly held her breath as Mum pulled open the door opposite and clattered downstairs to the lobby. Then she became aware of someone else breathing behind her.

With a grunt Molly flipped onto her back and saw, further down the corridor, Mrs Hellastroom in a yellow nightie, wielding a long shoehorn.

"This is just a dream, Mrs Hellastroom," whispered Molly, waving the woman away. "Go back to bed."

Mrs Hellastroom tramped back to her bedroom, and as she pulled the door shut Molly heard her hiss: "*Liar.*"

That word, and the sound of commotion from below — duelling voices and Gabriel mewling — caused a burst of guilt to bloom behind Molly's ribcage. As usual, she'd caused havoc: she'd helped blow up a hospital ward, turned Mr Wetherill into a fugitive, possibly upset the Excelsior's guests, and put her mother's business in jeopardy. As usual, Gabriel had endangered himself trying to bail her out. And what had Molly accomplished by sneaking out this evening, exactly? Zilch, that's what.

She heard Mr Banderfrith advising Mum to check

whether Molly was in her room. In a moment Molly was back on her feet, scampering for all she was worth, hoping she could get to her bedroom before Banderfrith could get to her.

The Queen of Liars

LOWRY HAD ONCE INVENTED A WORD FOR the state of frozen dithering that seizes you when you have too many things to do and you don't know where to start, or too many options and no way of choosing between them:

FRANTIPITATION

Back in her room, Molly frantipitated.

What to do first?

Trainers! She peeled them off. From downstairs came the faint strains of strife. It sounded as though Mum and Mr Banderfrith were physically fighting (which, given that Mum was nearly six feet tall and as strong as a horse, Molly would have quite liked to have seen).

Lamp! She switched on her bedside lamp.

Sweatshirt! She chucked her hooded sweatshirt into the corner of the room.

Light! She switched off the main light.

Pyjamas! She pulled on some pyjamas over her *Doris de Ville's Street Cleaning Crew* tee-shirt.

Bed —

Just as she was about to pull back the duvet, she heard a scratching at the door.

Then an impatient meow.

She ran to the door and opened it to Gabriel, who — "Ugh, Gabriel, that's disgusting!" — was sitting grandly on Mr Banderfrith's toupée as though it were the throne of a tribal king. Molly scooped up the mischievous-looking hairy creature with one hand, and Gabriel with the other.

"Thanks for saving me," she said, placing Gabriel on her desk chair. She took the wig to her built-in wardrobe, slid open the door — bracing herself in case books and boxes and maps toppled out and crushed her to death — and with a shiver of disgust she threw the wig onto her hill of frayed clothes. "Are you injured, Gabriel? Did you lose another life?"

He seemed OK. He scampered across the room and sprang onto the desk.

"I made a right royal mess of things tonight, Gabriel," Molly said. "Mr Wetherill blew up Howlfair

Infirmary and there's going to be a massive scandal tomorrow, and…" She heard something outside the room. She gasped. "Wait — *listen*."

Footsteps were nearing. Voices. Gabriel yawned and wandered behind the curtain. Only his tail, swishing, was visible.

Molly climbed into bed.

Rap! Rap! Rap! "Thompson! Open up!"

Mum's voice, quieter, apologetic: "Molly, are you there?"

"I said open up, deceiver!" Banderfrith roared.

"It's open!"

Banderfrith barged in, puce-faced, bowling-ball bald.

Behind him, at least a foot taller, Molly's mum looked drained and dejected.

"Behold the queen of liars!" he cried.

"Mr Banderfrith, don't be melodramatic," Mum said.

"I saw her sneaking into the guesthouse after dark — even though I heard you expressly order her to abide by the terms of her curfew." He pointed a trembling finger. "Do you deny it, girl?"

Molly looked at Mum, then at her accuser. "Um, perhaps you just *imagined* seeing me, Mr Banderfrith," she ventured.

"I'm not blind!" Mr Banderfrith guffawed. "I know what I saw — and I clearly saw you sneaking in."

She pulled up her duvet with its *Bride of Frankenstein* cover. It was time to take a gamble. Molly was pretty sure that Banderfrith had only *heard* her come in. So she said, "What was I wearing?"

The old man scowled. "Wearing?"

"You said you saw me clearly. What was I wearing?" Mum looked at Mr Banderfrith with interest.

"I don't always pay attention to small details like clothing..." he spluttered.

"No idea what colours I was wearing? Whether I had on a coat?"

"Yes, a coat! You had on a coat."

Molly felt wretched and smug. "My coat's in the wash," she said. "Isn't it, Mum? After I leaned against that wall you painted."

Mum nodded slowly and narrowed her eyes at her guest.

"What, you only have one coat?" Banderfrith cried. "I find that hard to believe!"

Mum's voice was low and dangerous. "Mr Banderfrith, did you or did you not see Molly in the lobby? Because Molly promised me solemnly that she'll never again sneak out of the guesthouse — and I trust her."

Molly squirmed with guilt.

"I may not have seen her," said Banderfrith, "but I definitely *heard* her..."

"First you said you saw her. Now you say you didn't see her." Mum cracked her knuckles. "Well, now we've cleared that matter up, let's move onto the next topic of discussion — your wig."

"Cleared the matter up!" Banderfrith gasped. "Surely you don't believe..."

"Mr Banderfrith, if we are to live together harmoniously under my roof, you will need to be more selective about what you accuse Molly of." She inspected a sharp jade-painted nail. Molly saw it glint dangerously. "Maybe cut back to one accusation a week?"

Banderfrith frantipitated.

"Or maybe," he said at last, "I should consider moving elsewhere."

Mum seemed to buckle a little; she'd tangled with Mr Banderfrith before, but he'd never threatened to leave.

"Mr Banderfrith, you've lived here for over a decade."

"I think I'll take a look at some other guesthouses tomorrow morning," said Banderfrith. "I've heard the Blowbridge Tavern is good."

"Yeah, if you like rats," Molly blurted.

"Maybe the staff there will treat me with respect."

Banderfrith chuckled to himself, a chuckle like a car starting on a cold day. "At least they *have* staff."

"I beg your pardon?" said Mum.

"I've noticed that all of your previous staff have disappeared," Banderfrith sneered. "Oh, but I suppose you don't *need* staff when you hardly have any guests, eh? And I suppose you don't think five residents are worth heating the place for — or is it that you're having problems paying your heating bills and getting your ancient boiler fixed?"

Molly realized why Banderfrith was being so bold. He'd figured out that Mum was struggling to keep the Excelsior afloat. He knew she couldn't afford to lose another long-term resident.

"The heating has been cutting off occasionally, but... Mr Banderfrith, let's talk this through. Maybe come to an arrangement."

Banderfrith sneaked a sly peek at Molly. "What kind of arrangement?"

Mum shook her head. "Maybe a discount on our vegetarian specials? Or —"

Banderfrith cut her short. "I wish for your idle daughter, from this day forth ... to clean my room."

"Sorry?" Mum yelped.

"You're kidding!" Molly gasped.

"Every morning at six-thirty, while I take my constitutional," Banderfrith went on. "Starting tomorrow."

Mum shook her head. "I'm sorry, Mr Banderfrith, but I can't agree to that."

"Then I will find a new place to live, and I will make sure that everyone in Howlfair knows of the outrageous indignities I've suffered in this unstaffed, unheated den of hair thieves." His eyes wandered over to the desk, then to Molly's wardrobe. "I wouldn't be surprised if my stolen toupée were somewhere in this very room..."

Molly's eyes widened.

Banderfrith moved towards the cupboard.

Molly couldn't let Banderfrith and Mum see that wig.

She couldn't let Mum know that Banderfrith's accusations were correct; that she had sneaked out of the Excelsior.

She squawked: *"I'll do it!"*

Banderfrith stopped and turned. Mum looked aghast.

"What was that?" Banderfrith cooed delightedly, cupping his ear. "Louder, please."

"I said I'll do it!"

Mum frowned heavily. "Molly, he can't make you clean his room. He's already wrongly accused you of sneaking out —"

"It's OK, Mum." Molly tried to swallow her disgust. "Maybe I *should* do more to help you keep the place tidy."

"See, Mrs Thompson — sometimes it takes a *man* to impose discipline in a household!" Banderfrith clapped his little hands. "I expect my room to be gleamingly clean by seven a.m. every morning, Sundays included. And if my hairpiece isn't waiting for me on my desk when I return from my walk around town tomorrow, I will make myself a replacement." His damp gaze slid slowly towards Molly. *"From your cat."*

The Snake

WHEN MR BANDERFRITH HAD GONE, MOLLY and her mother lapsed into stunned awkwardness. Eventually Mum spoke.

"You didn't have to offer to clean his room. I shouldn't have let you."

"But he's got us over a barrel, hasn't he? He's figured out that we can't pay our bills."

"Yes," Mum said miserably. "Any day now the boiler's going to go kaput. God knows what's going to happen when winter hits."

"If we give Mr Banderfrith something to feel smug about now, maybe he'll be a bit more understanding when the boiler goes."

"It's a very kind thing you offered to do," said Mum. "And by the way, I didn't believe it for a second. About you sneaking out."

Molly stared down at her duvet. "I've never

understood why Banderfrith hates me so much," she said, to change the subject.

"Ever since Dad died he's seemed very keen to keep you in line," said Mum. "Maybe he thinks you need a disciplinarian father figure."

"Mr Banderfrith, a father figure?" said Molly. "Yikes."

"I'm off to bed," said Mum. "Remember to pick up Banderfrith's key from the office tomorrow morning, and let me know if you find his nightmarish hair. And listen — you won't have to be Mr Banderfrith's maid for long. I'll find a way to win him round."

Once Mum had left, Molly's guilt deepened.

"I broke my promise to Mum, I nearly drove Banderfrith out of the guesthouse, Lowry nearly got shot, I've constantly been trying to convince my friends that ghouls are about to kill us, and I've got a stolen wig in my wardrobe," she said to her cat. "Gabriel, tell me the truth. Am I a bad person?"

Gabriel's tail appeared from between the curtains over Molly's desk, and swished.

Molly nodded. "A snake," she said. "You're right. I'm a snake."

Molly the snake.

Molly the recalcitrant brat.

Molly the Queen of Liars.

"Gabriel, I'm going to make it up to Mum. I'm going to try worrying about *her* instead of panicking about ghouls. Do you hear me? Snake no more!"

Her cat emerged from between the curtains and meowed. Molly frowned at him.

"Go on then. Let's hear your idea."

He sneezed.

"You think I should make a new promise to Mum, and this time make sure I keep it?" Molly said. She scratched her chin. "Actually, that's a pretty good suggestion, Gabriel."

He trundled back behind his curtains, looking up at the stars beyond the window.

"I'll do it, Gabriel," said Molly. "I'll think of a promise. Starting tomorrow, I'm going to be a new and greatly improved person."

For a moment Molly thought about the demon who'd infiltrated her dreams earlier that summer, and who hadn't visited her since Molly had triumphed over the monsters she'd met in the crypts below Loonchance Manor. The demon who'd claimed that Molly, one day, would open the gates of Hell and release all its fiends.

Lady Orgella, the Mistress of Ghouls.

Molly forced herself to remember what the demon had called her.

She hadn't called her a brat, or a liar, or a snake. She'd called her something very different, something almost affectionate:

My own dear, doomed Molly.

Gabriel poked his head through the curtains and hissed as though he'd seen Lady Orgella herself flicker into view behind Molly, reaching to caress the girl's frenzy of dark curls.

The thought gave Molly the chills, and she span around to see if there was anyone there.

Nobody.

She looked at Gabriel, who stood with hair on end, eyes narrow.

"I'm not *'her Molly'*, Gabriel," she said, putting a hand to the cat's little face. "And I never will be."

Gabriel looked away, as though soothed with her assurance.

Or perhaps he read something in her face that forced him to avert his gaze. Perhaps Gabriel could divine something in Molly's future that she could not yet see.

Maid Molly

THE FOLLOWING MORNING MOLLY SNOOZED through her six-a.m. alarm, waking twenty minutes late for her cleaning duties.

"Oh bums!"

So much for new and improved.

In haste she dressed, pulling on a bobbled sweater over her *Doris de Ville's Street Cleaning Crew* tee-shirt. She put Mr Banderfrith's glossy toupée in a plastic bag. From her window she saw Banderfrith strolling past the cemetery in a different wig. She scowled. Gabriel meowed at her as she headed across the room.

"I'll be fine, Gabriel. I'm just cleaning Banderfrith's bedroom." She paused at the door, took the wig out of the bag and waved it at Gabriel. "Hey, want to say goodbye to your friend?"

Gabriel shuddered.

*　*　*

Mum, Molly discovered when she went to get the room key, hadn't gone to bed last night. She'd fallen asleep in her office. Now she lay with her head on her desk, hair dramatically splayed, surrounded by bills and receipts; some were tangled in her hair. As Molly made her way into the room, Mum stirred and looked up, red-eyed.

"Molly, what time is it?"

"Six-thirty," said Molly. "Why are you still here?"

"Stayed up late sorting a few things out. The usual stuff."

"Money stuff?"

"It's official — we're broke," Mum said. "Can't pay the bills. Can't fix the boiler. Can't..." She rubbed her eyes. "Sorry, Molly — I didn't mean to be abrupt. I just thought maybe some of our financial difficulties would vanish if I spent all night pushing receipts around my desk before falling asleep on my calculator. Amazingly, they did not."

Molly chewed her lip. "Do you think we'll have to sell the guesthouse?"

"Sell the Excelsior?" Mum looked up, alarmed. "I don't... It's been in the family forever, and... No, Molly, no! That's not an option. Anyway, who would we sell it to?"

"It's OK, Mum — I was just wondering what our Plan B was."

"We don't have a Plan B," Mum said. "Or a Plan A."

She yawned and closed her eyes and leaned sideways. Molly grabbed her and she awoke with a gasp.

"Mum, you need a good night's sleep."

Mum shook her head. "We need *guests*. We need tourists to come to Howlfair. We need to stop advertising ourselves as Britain's Most Horrifying Town, and try to get *normal* people to come here for *normal* holidays." She raised a fist, as though she were going to bang it on the desk. Instead she lifted her hand to remove a receipt from her red-gold hair. "We need a miracle."

Mum and Dad had always been a double act; they'd made up for each other's shortcomings. Together, they'd managed to make the Excelsior Guesthouse work. But since Dad's death, Mum often seemed lost, unsure, prone to frantipitation. And although Molly longed to help, she was painfully aware that she often got in the way.

"Howlfair," Mum said, "needs to become famous for something other than having more scary legends than anywhere in the known universe."

"What like?"

"I don't know. Scones? Flapjacks?" She narrowed her eyes thoughtfully at the ceiling. *"Howlfair — Town of Flapjacks. Town of a Thousand Flapjacks."*

"World's Scariest Flapjacks," ventured Molly.

"Or maybe jam! International town of … jam." She sighed and stood, brushing receipts from her hair. "I'm going to go and make some vegetarian breakfasts for our miserable guests to complain about."

"Howlfair! World's most miserable vegetarians," said Molly. She took a key from Mum's desk and unlocked the spare key cupboard. "Right, Mum, I'm off to clean Mr Banderfrith's room," she said. "If it turns out to be full of mannequins that look like him, and they're all wearing wigs, and I die from horror — it was nice knowing you."

There were sticky notes all over Mr Banderfrith's bedroom, instructing Molly to perform various feats. Like stand on tiptoes and clean objects she could barely reach:

Dust trophies on top shelf

Or shift heavy furniture:

Clean skirting board behind armchair

Molly dropped Banderfrith's hairpiece next to his old-fashioned lamp. She switched the lamp on. It flared, and then the bulb died with a *pop!*

"Oh, crud!" she hissed. "One more thing for Banderfrith to moan about."

Suddenly an idea came to her. "Wait a minute…"

She picked up her can of beeswax spray and aimed it at the lamp. The can was the wrong way round, so when she pressed the top it sprayed over her shoulder. Molly didn't notice. She was thinking.

"I've got it!" she said to the old man's wig. "The next mystery I need to solve! It's right under my nose!"

She opened the window and shook out Mr Banderfrith's oval rug. She frowned out at the valley, and peered down the side of the building towards the deliveries area below. Past the monstrous, thick vine — livid green, studded with thorns the size of vultures' beaks — which climbed alongside Banderfrith's window.

"And a promise," she whispered. "There's a promise I can make to Mum!"

A *big* promise — the biggest promise she could think of.

She shut the window and raced through the rest of the cleaning, leaving the room gleaming and smelling of beeswax.

Solemn Scout

"CAN YOU TELL LOWRY NOT TO PHONE SO early?" Mum said as Molly skidded into the office. "She'll wake people up."

Molly's muscles had started aching from her harsh cleaning duties. She rubbed her shoulder.

"Lowry? When did she call?" Molly walked to the wall-mounted phone.

"Just after seven. She was wittering about some sort of miracle. You can't phone her back — it's incoming calls only."

Molly replaced the receiver. "They cut us off?"

Mum nodded.

"I'll call for her in a bit," said Molly. "Anyway..."

"I hope this miracle of Lowry's is a good one. A lottery win, maybe, accompanied by a sudden urge to rescue the Excelsior."

"Lowry's last miracle was teaching her dog to count

to one," said Molly. "But listen — you know how I'm always getting into trouble solving mysteries?"

Mum looked up. "What have you done now?"

"Nothing!" said Molly. *Other than blow up a hospital and nearly ruin the Excelsior by making Banderfrith leave.* "The thing is, I've found a new mystery to solve." She took a breath. "How to save the Excelsior."

Mum appeared dubious. "Really?"

"Mum, I've never failed to solve a mystery in my life. So maybe I should use my famous mystery-solving skills to solve a mystery that doesn't involve…"

"Vampires?" said Mum.

"Yes, or…"

"Or digging up dirt on the locals so that the whole town petitions me to make you stop?"

"Yes, that sort of thing…"

"Or sneaking out at midnight and ending up in hospital after breaking into Loonchance Manor for reasons we still haven't discussed?"

"Exactly!" said Molly. "It will be a completely humdrum mystery-solving quest in which nobody will get injured and I will be victorious."

The way Mum was studying her made Molly feel weird.

"Uh, Mum?"

"You look like your dad used to look," Mum said.

"When he was proposing some mad plan, and I'd ask whether he really thought he could pull it off. He'd always do a boy-scout salute and say *I solemnly promise*. And he'd always keep his word."

"I'm not proposing a *mad* plan. I'm proposing a *sensible* plan."

Mum frowned at Molly for some time. "Famous mystery-solving troublemaker Molly Thompson is going to find a way to save our guesthouse ... without causing any trouble?"

Molly raised three fingers to her temple. A scout salute. "I solemnly promise."

Corpse in a Car

LITTLE VALLEY DRIVE, NEAR HOWLFAIR
Astrology Tower, was so named because its
eight slate-roofed houses surrounded a small oval
green that dipped in the middle to form a little
valley. The houses — bungalows, antique and pastel
painted — sagged in the middle like shy smiles. The
two big windows on each house front were kindly
eyes, rheumy with condensation. Although Little
Valley Drive was near the busiest shopping streets
of Howlfair, it had the hush of classroom gossip; an
encompassing ring of darksbane trees — gnarly,
twisted, like giants magically frozen halfway through
their morning stretches — absorbed the discordant
music of town centre traffic. Molly loved coming here,
not least because her best friend lived at number three.

She hadn't been here for a few weeks. Mrs Evans
had been angry with Molly for poisoning Lowry

with a home-made werewolf potion that summer. But Lowry claimed that her dad had talked her mum into forgiving her.

Lowry wasn't home, though, when Molly arrived at Little Valley Drive. Molly had barely emerged from the belt of trees when the Evans family car — with all the family inside — rattled past her, waking a golden flurry of autumn leaves.

Lowry was slumped with her head against the window and her eyes rolled back in her head and her tongue hanging out. As the car rounded the oval green, Lowry pitched sideways and collapsed stiffly onto her sister. Molly waved but nobody saw her except Sheila, the Evans's English bull terrier puppy, who grinned at Molly from the big boot.

The car disappeared, heading towards the main road. Moments later Molly heard a brief bugling of brakes. Then the car reversed and rocked to a stop a few metres from Molly. There was shouting. Shamefaced and grumbling, Lowry got out, a gingham shirt tied around her waist. The car grunted back into motion and Lowry, spotting Molly on the pavement, broke into a grin and waved.

"Molly!" she shouted, jogging over. "Oh, I'm glad you're here. It's been an ordeal of a morning. We were going on a trip to get lovely new school clothes, and then I discovered that only Frances is getting new clothes, and — can you believe it? — they're giving me her cast-offs! The only new things I'm getting are socks! Socks, by God!" She briefly raised her fists to the heavens. "So I said I wished I was dead, and Frances said she wished I was dead too, and I said fine! I'm dead. You'll have to carry me round the shops. So I was pretending to be dead in the car — did you see me? I was superb. Rigor mortis, lolling tongue — the works. Then Dad looks in his rear-view mirror and... Hey, did you get my message this morning?"

"That's why I'm here," said Molly. "To hear about a miracle."

Lowry clapped excitedly, and nodded towards her bungalow. "First, let me go inside and call Felicity so she can meet us at Wetherill's shop," she said. "I'll tell you on the way."

"Wetherill's shop?" Molly's spirits sank.

"You promised you'd visit Carl, remember?" said Lowry, taking out her keys. "I get the feeling Wetherill specifically wanted you to see him."

"But I'd rather be dead than see Carl," grumbled Molly. "Rigor mortis, lolling tongue, the works."

"You won't want to be dead when you hear my miraculous news," said Lowry. "Howlfair is about to change forever."

Country Wonders

MOLLY AND LOWRY LIVED IN THE SAME town — and they lived in different towns.

Take West Circuit Street, for example, this grey-cobbled northward road, one of the three long roads that formed the Circuit. As the girls passed posh shops (Shelby Dyre — Bespoke Tailoring; Randleman's Fine Antiques), salons (the Grey Lady Boutique), eateries (the Manglewulf Bistro), each establishment brought to Molly's mind the scary legends linked to it, legends dating back to Howlfair's Dark Days. Lowry, on the other hand, knew by heart the menus and the best places to buy chocolate or sparkly shoes. Same places; different experiences.

And whenever the girls passed elegant town houses with basement kitchens and iron-railed balconies, Lowry nosily leered into the living rooms, waving shamelessly if one of the residents caught her looking.

But Molly's gaze picked out the building's historical details. The plaques. The carvings that witch-hunters had made on houses thought to harbour hags. The faded scorch marks that ran down some house fronts, which Molly knew had been made by terrified servants in times of yore, sent quaking onto balconies to tip boiling pitch over gangs of midnight visitors (feared to be ghouls or vampires) gathering hungrily, by moonlight, below.

Lowry saw snooty hotel doormen whose hats made her giggle. But Molly's gaze ranged higher, to the flags that rippled above the doormen's heads, flags displaying the Howlfair insignia and the coded motto that Molly had only recently deciphered as *If Howlfair Falls, The Whole World Falls.*

"So listen to my miraculous news," Lowry said as they walked. "Apparently a journalist from *Country Wonders* magazine is coming to do a feature on Howlfair."

Molly stumbled over a cobble. "*Country Wonders*! Flipping heck, Lowry!"

"What, you've heard of it?"

"Of course! They feature a different town or village in every issue, and they write about the history and the people, the shops, the restaurants and houses, local myths and legends…"

"How do you know all this?"

"I've got every issue," said Molly. "I like to see if any other town in England has better myths and legends than Howlfair."

"And?"

"They don't."

"Well, anyway, Dad says that when a town's featured in *Country Wonders*, it instantly becomes a tourist hot spot and turns into Monte Carlo or something."

"Depends on who's writing the article," said Molly. "There's this one writer, Gordon Lovage, who makes every place he visits look *amazing*. But these two others, Lucinda and Orson Corches — a brother and sister — are really vile. They always make fun of the towns they visit."

"Ah, that explains why Dad's so jumpy. His boss wants him to be a tour guide for whatever journalists they send us. And they're going to send us the nasty ones, aren't they?"

"Not necessarily," said Molly. "Even if they do, maybe your dad'll win them over, and he'll be a hero."

"This is my dad we're talking about, Molly. When he's under pressure he collapses like a depressed soufflé. But anyway, it's still exciting, don't you think? Howlfair might become world-famous!"

The girls turned onto Longmorrow Lane, where

Wetherill's Weaponry Store nestled between other gift shops.

"I'm not looking forward to this," said Molly.

"What, Howlfair becoming world-famous?"

"No — seeing Carl Grobman," said Molly. "I'm not good at dealing with people who've tried to kill me."

"It's one of those life skills they don't teach us at school," Lowry said. "Listen, Carl's had a pretty cruddy life. He's never had friends, and he spent years in Furlock's orphanage getting brainwashed. Maybe we should give him a second chance."

"What, a second chance to kill me?"

"It's hard for me, too," said Lowry. "He nearly killed my best friend. And I've got the added problem of worrying about turning into a werewolf if I get too angry with him."

Molly rolled her eyes. Then she spotted Felicity waiting near the tall tangle tree near the shop, her severe diagonal fringe slicing through a frown.

"Yo, Felicity!" Lowry said. "Cripes, if looks could kill. What's up?"

"Parents are playing up again," grumbled Felicity. "Maybe the sight of Grobman's miserable little face will make me feel better about my life." She looked at Molly. "Are you ready to face him?"

"No," Molly mumbled.

81

"Just do this one favour for old Wetherill," Felicity said, grabbing Molly's arm and tugging her towards the shop. "Then, if you want, you'll never have to speak to Grobman ever again."

For some reason, this thought made Molly feel even worse.

Wetherill's Weaponry Store

A STREAKY VEIL OF CONDENSATION ON THE long front window obscured the view of the rows of fake stakes and silver bullets and ghoul flares. The OPEN sign hung on the door, which meant that Carl Grobman was manning the shop.

Back in the Dark Days of Howlfair history, when the townsfolk believed that the Ethelhael Valley was full of monsters, this store sold real monster-hunting weapons. Nowadays it was a tourist gift shop that sold toys and replicas (and local fudge). There were, however, rumours that Mr Wetherill had an old stash of *real* weapons hidden on the premises. Moreover, it was whispered that Wetherill (along with a few other local cranks, such as farmer Thomas Digby, or Gilda Giddimus, landlady of the Stake House Inn) actually believed that the old legends of Howlfair's monsters were true.

Recently, Molly had learned that the legends *were* true. And those rumours about Mr Wetherill were true as well. What's more, she'd discovered that Wetherill had once belonged to a secret monster-hunting group known as the Guild of Asphodel.

About ten years ago the Guild of Asphodel had set out to discover once and for all whether the fiends from Howlfair's horror stories, fiends that the legends said had been defeated by brave townsfolk, were still hiding in the valley. Wetherill had told Molly that the Guild disbanded after failing to find any trace of monsters. He refused to name any of the other members. Molly suspected there was a lot more to the story.

The tinny sound of a witch's cackle crackled from a small speaker as Molly pushed open the shop door.

Beyond the displays of novelty weapons and the hideous mannequins, Carl Grobman sat hunched behind the mahogany counter, miniaturized by one of Wetherill's grubby gargantuan greatcoats. He was frowning from beneath his greasy black fringe at a splayed newspaper, occasionally blinking his sleepless eyes. Upon hearing the witch's cackle, he leaped up.

The shop was freezing. Molly's breath turned to steam.

"There's been an explosion in the infirmary!" Carl

croaked in a voice that suggested he hadn't spoken to anyone in a while. He threw the newspaper over the counter, and Felicity caught it. "Mr Wetherill was there, but now he's not, and I don't know what's happened…" He flicked a glance at Molly. "Hi, Molly."

Molly muttered a greeting, her face heating despite the cold. She joined Felicity and looked at the front page of *The Ethelhael Panopticon*.

MYSTERY FIREBALL ENGULFS HOWLFAIR INFIRMARY

"Apparently the Grim Reaper was sighted," Carl said fearfully, chewing a fingernail. "The police are treating it as some sort of practical joke, but Mr Wetherill has vanished and the police are concerned for his safety…"

"He's fine," said Lowry, taking a toy ghoul flare from a shelf and hefting it in her palm. "We've spoken to him. He asked us to come here and tell you he's OK."

"Ha ha, it says here that Mrs Marrible is one hundred and seventy-six years old," said Felicity, flipping through the paper.

Carl ignored her. "How come you've seen him?"

Lowry put the flare back on the shelf. "We went to

the infirmary last night in disguise to tell him about an old prophecy, but everyone freaked out because I was disguised as Death, and we went to the Kroglin Mausoleum, and now Mr Wetherill's staying with a friend and everything's OK and the ghouls aren't back."

Carl looked at Molly. "Has Lowry gone mad?"

"No madder than usual," sighed Felicity, proceeding through the paper. "Hey, what's this?"

Molly jolted when she saw the picture:

"PHANTOM" FURLOCK SIGHTED

Beneath the headline was a picture of a glaring, skull-faced man in a military jacket, into the folds of which he had tucked one hand. Molly hadn't seen that face, that jacket, *that monstrous moustache*, since the night Benton Furlock, with the help of Carl Grobman, who he'd brainwashed into serving him, had lured her to Loonchance Manor in the hope of killing her.

Benton Furlock was a creepy businessman and philanthropist who'd hoped to be voted Mayor of Howlfair in the August elections. He'd run the orphanage where Carl used to live. Molly had discovered that Furlock had been blackmailing locals into giving him money for his lavish election campaign. A servant of the demon Lady Orgella, the legendary Mistress of Ghouls, Benton Furlock had figured out how to summon the ghouls from one of Howlfair's creepiest folk tales, and had been using the ghouls to terrify people. His fantastical plan was to help Lady Orgella turn the town into a gateway between Hell and earth, and eventually make Howlfair the capital of a new Hell, in which Furlock would serve as Prime Minister.

Molly had gained control of the ghouls and convinced them to turn against Furlock if he didn't leave Howlfair. Apart from Wallace Wetherill, who'd believed Molly's story, nobody else in town knew that Howlfair had nearly been taken over by a demon-worshipping madman with a private army of ghouls.

Nobody else knew why Benton Furlock had disappeared just before the announcement of the election results.

Now the ghouls had vanished, and Benton Furlock was in the newspapers again.

"'Furlock has been missing from Howlfair since losing the mayoral elections in August, after Wallace Wetherill of Wetherill's Weaponry Store persuaded fellow members of Howlfair Worker's Union to withdraw their vote for him,'" Felicity read. "'Police have been investigating his disappearance — but recently a number of residents claim to have caught sight of Mr Furlock at night…'"

"He's come back for us!" said Carl in a trembly voice. "He's going to get revenge on us for what we did!"

"Well, how about that, Thompson!" Felicity said to Molly. "Looks like Grobman's just as paranoid as you."

Carl said, "Paranoid?"

Lowry took the newspaper from Felicity and squinted at the photograph with a shudder. "Maybe paranoid is too strong a word," she said to Carl, "but Molly *has* spent quite a lot of time lately acting like ghouls are about to leap out from behind every tree, which is perfectly understandable given that we were nearly eaten by ghouls over the summer holidays…"

Molly opened her mouth to say something, but she was momentarily distracted by the arrival of some shoppers at the door: a middle-aged woman and three youngsters in hoodies. She watched as they gathered outside, peering in as though trying to decide whether it was safe to enter.

The sound of Lowry shouting brought Molly back to her senses.

"Why are you even trying to stick up for her, Grobman? You're the one who nearly got her killed!

She didn't even want to come here and see you, did you, Molly?"

Molly looked round.

"I know I nearly got her killed, and I'll never forgive myself," Carl said. He looked utterly wretched. "But I don't think you should make her feel like she's being paranoid just because she's worried about ghouls. Not after what happened."

"After what *you* did to her," said Felicity.

"I'm sorry!" cried Carl, putting his head in his hands. "I wish I could take it back!"

The woman outside stood frozen, watching through the door's windowpane as Carl and Lowry and Felicity argued.

"We'd better go," said Molly, feeling an unwelcome stab of sadness on behalf of Carl Grobman, the friend who'd tried to arrange her murder. "Carl has customers."

As Lowry held the door open for the woman and her chain of hooded munchkins, and the girls filtered out, Molly turned to see Carl lift his head from his hands with pathetic weariness and wipe the back of his hand across his eyes.

The sight was almost enough to tempt Molly to forgive him.

But then the question of how Carl could betray her

started to ache afresh behind Molly's ribcage.

The feeling swelled and swirled and began to exert a gravitational pull...

"Come on, Thompson!" said Lowry.

She caught her breath and followed her friends down Longmorrow Lane.

Flipping Nora!

"**W**HY DID YOU HAVE TO EMBARRASS ME like that in front of Carl?" Molly said. "Saying I'm being paranoid? Like I don't already feel like enough of a doofus around him..."

"Why on earth would you care what Carl Grobman thinks of you?" said Felicity, reaching up to bat the overhanging branch of a tangle tree as though it were a volleyball.

"I wasn't trying to embarrass you, Molly," Lowry said, fanning herself with the newspaper she'd neglected to return to Carl. "I just wanted him to know that thanks to him, you've been very jumpy and weird lately."

"Also, Molly," said Felicity thoughtfully, "I've noticed that you don't say 'Flipping Nora!' any more."

"She's right!" Lowry confirmed. "I haven't heard you say 'Flipping Nora!' for flipping months."

"What are you talking about?" Molly said. "I say it all the time!"

"I hate to bring this up," said Felicity, "but how do we know that you're not a ghoul impersonating Molly? I mean, you've stopped using your famous catchphrase..."

"Then of course I must be a ghoul!" Molly cried, startling a passing mother and her child. "Because who doesn't know that ghouls hate catchphrases!"

She moved to cross the road. She needed to get away from Lowry and Felicity and from their silly accusations.

"Hey, come back, Miss Sensitive," said Lowry. "We're only teasing."

"Take Felicity to Cakes 'n' Shakes and tell her your news about *Country Wonders* magazine," Molly said. "I'm going home to help my mum."

Closing her ears to Lowry's objections, Molly hurried towards the Circuit. Back to the guesthouse she'd solemnly promised to save.

A visitor was waiting for her there. A visitor — and a miracle.

Tour Guide Wanted

MOLLY COULD HEAR MUM TALKING IN THE lounge as she arrived in the hallway. She couldn't hear what Mum was saying, only that she was speaking in the kind of accent you'd normally expect to be accompanied by the tinkle of champagne glasses. As it happened, it was accompanied by the sound of the lounge's broken radiators whining like alley cats, and, briefly, by the sound of Mrs Hellastroom (lurking on the stairs with Mr Banderfrith) burping into her sleeve.

After Mum's voice came another voice. A familiar voice with a calm Caribbean accent.

Molly frowned at Banderfrith and Mrs Hellastroom and poked her head around the lounge door.

"Ah, Molly!" gushed Mum. "Come and meet the mayor!"

And there he was in the lounge of the Excelsior,

standing by a coffee table: the Mayor of Howlfair. Lawrence de Ville. The husband (incidentally) of Molly's form tutor, Doris de Ville. Wearing a dark green suit that was too long for his short frame, too narrow for his shoulders. He had the droopy, sad face of a bulldog left in a car. A sprig of greying beard.

"Hello, Mr Mayor," said Molly, waving unnecessarily as she went over.

"Molly's usually much better dressed, Mr Mayor," Mum lied. The mayor looked sceptical, so Mum started improvizing. "She's been out auditioning for a part in a play. The part of ... an urchin."

"You're an actress?" the mayor said to Molly. "Doris has always described you as a quiet, shy girl..."

"Quiet and shy?" Mum spluttered. "Molly *can* be quiet at times, but she's certainly not *shy*. No sir. No siree Bob."

"Shy or not, Mrs Thompson, Molly's the one my wife has recommended for the magazine job," the mayor said.

"Magazine job?" Molly blurted.

"*Country Wonders* magazine!" Mum yelped. "They're featuring Howlfair in an upcoming issue!"

"Molly, this is big news," said the mayor, while Molly tried to look as though she were hearing it for the first time. "Very big news. A favourable write-up in *Country Wonders* could give the Howlfair tourist trade the things it so desperately lacks."

"Like tourists?" said Molly.

"Yes," Mr de Ville said. "And trade."

Molly said, "And ... Mrs de Ville recommended me?"

"She said you were the obvious choice."

Molly blinked. "Why?"

"Because apparently you know this town's history and stories better than anybody on earth. And also — you're a child! Nothing pulls at a journalist's heartstrings like a poor waif-like girl of — what are you, ten? Six?"

"Twelve."

"The thing is, Molly, there's a chance that the magazine might send us some ... difficult journalists. But even difficult journalists would warm to a *child*! Especially one who looks like she's just climbed out of a skip."

"Not sure that's called for," said Mum.

"We could definitely exploit this whole urchin angle," the mayor said. "Perhaps you could wear these shabby rags when you show the journalists around? Maybe wear just one shoe! How would you feel about having grime smeared on your face?"

Mum cleared her throat. "Molly, what are your thoughts?"

"About the grime?"

"About any of it."

Molly scratched her head. "Sounds like quite a big responsibility."

"It is," said the mayor darkly. "Our town is going to sink without a trace if we don't find a way to attract tourists, and this is, frankly, our last hope." He stifled a sudden sob.

"Molly, the mayor says that if you were to volunteer to be our tour guide, he'd make sure that the *Country Wonders* journalist stays here — in the Excelsior," said Mum. "And he'd send some people over to fix the place up. *To fix the place up*, Molly. Wouldn't that be miraculous?"

A radiator gurgled. A pipe, somewhere over the mayor's head, let out a deathly groan.

So that was why Mum was acting so weird. In one fell swoop, all the Excelsior's problems could be washed away. Repairs. Renovations. A journalist from *Country Wonders* staying under this very roof. A glowing feature about the guesthouse in a famous magazine.

A curtain fell off a broken rail.

"I have noticed that the place could do with a … touch-up," said the mayor.

From outside the lounge door, Mrs Hellastroom and Mr Banderfrith both snorted.

"Molly, I need you to be honest with me," said the mayor. "Do you think you can make Howlfair look like somewhere that normal people would want to visit for their holidays?" He leaned forward in his chair. His suit creaked. "Could you save our town?"

"And our guesthouse," Mum mumbled inadvertently. She looked up. "But there's no pressure, Molly. The decision is yours."

Molly looked at Mum and grinned. A way to save the Excelsior had fallen into her lap — and all she needed to do was show one or two possibly cranky journalists around her town!

She was pretty sure she could do *that*.

Briefly she gave Mum a scout's salute. She saw relief flood Mum's features.

"Mr Mayor," she said, "you bet your bum I'll do it."

After the mayor had left and Mr Banderfrith and Mrs Hellastroom had been sent back to their rooms, Molly and Mum sat down by the fire with mugs of tea.

Mum leaned forward and put her hand on Molly's arm. Her eyes were wide and green and gleaming. A strand of rose-gold hair was in her tea. "Molly, if you don't want to do this, that's fine."

97

"It doesn't sound too hard, Mum," Molly said. "And I promised, remember?"

"I can tell that you're nervous about all this responsibility," said Mum. "All you need is a bit of confidence, and maybe some grime smeared on your face…"

"*Mum*."

"You can do it. If I didn't think you could, I wouldn't let you try."

The phone rang and Mum leaped up to answer it. When she returned, she looked thrilled and petrified.

"That was the mayor," she said. "He's just got off the phone to *Country Wonders* magazine."

"And?"

"And they love the idea of having a young girl as their journalist's tour guide."

"They do?"

"That's not all. Their journalist will be moving into our guesthouse *next week* to start writing his feature."

"Next week! Wait — did the mayor tell who'll be writing the feature?"

"Someone named Gordon something…"

"Gordon Lovage!" Molly coughed. "Blinking flip, he's the nicest journalist at *Country Wonders*!"

"Well, the mayor wants you to have lunch with him at the Walnut Whatnot tomorrow. One o'clock."

"Tomorrow!"

"Fanciest restaurant in Howlfair."

Molly felt faint. The magazine was sending Gordon Lovage to write a glowing feature about her town!

Molly was going to save Howlfair. Again. And this time she wouldn't need to be trapped in any ghoul-infested crypts.

What's more, she was going to rescue the Excelsior Guesthouse. Just like she'd promised.

"What are you thinking?" said Mum.

"I'm thinking that I need to go through my *Country Wonders* collection and read everything Gordon Lovage's ever written."

"Good plan, Stan," Mum said. "Molly — I think our worries are over. I think this is the miracle we've been waiting for."

Dressing for Whatnot

"MOLLY, ARE YOU SURE YOU WANT TO do this?" said Lowry. "It just seems so daredevil-ish and risky…"

They were in Lowry's bedroom the following morning, Molly on the bed, Lowry sifting through the clothes in her wardrobe.

"I didn't have a choice," said Molly. "Mr Wetherill told the mayor I should do it."

"No — I meant borrowing one of my dresses. You're not really a fancy gown kind of gal. You're more a…" She chewed her lip, then gestured at Molly with both hands. "You're … *that*. Your style is … that. That thing you're wearing."

"My dad's old Iron Maiden tee-shirt?"

"Exactly. Molly Thompson is the kind of girl who actually goes out in her dad's old Iron Maiden tee-shirt."

"Oh — I forgot to say!" Molly sat up. "It's Gordon Lovage who's coming to Howlfair, not those nasty Corches siblings."

"The really nice journalist? Cor and crikey with a side order of blimeys, Molly, that's brilliant!"

A voice from the open doorway. "What's brilliant?" It was Lowry's dad.

"Come in, Dad. The mayor's asked Molly to be the tour guide for your *Country Wonders* journalist. So you're off the hook! And get this — they're sending Gordon Lovage!"

Mr Evans stepped into the room, scratching his sandy hair.

He leaned against the wall. "Gordon Lovage," he said to himself. "They sent *Gordon Blinking Lovage* to Howlfair. Even *I* could've impressed Gordon Lovage. Almost makes me wish *I'd* volunteered to be his tour guide."

"Nah, you'd have found a way to bungle it," said Lowry.

"Yes, you're probably right."

"Molly's just off to meet him at the Walnut Whatnot and get treated to a seventeen-course lunch."

"Well, make sure you use the right cutlery for the right course," Mr Evans said to Molly.

"It's *Gordon Lovage*, Dad! She could accidentally

throw her chilled beetroot and truffle soup all over his head and he'd still write a good article about Howlfair."

"Molly, promise me something," said Lowry's dad.

"Yes, Mr Evans?"

"Promise me you'll put as much energy into this tour guide business as you do into solving local mysteries."

"Course!" Molly said.

"And try to make Howlfair sound like somewhere that normal people will want to visit."

"Definitely, Mr Evans."

"Because I know you enjoy talking about our local legends concerning vampires and ghouls and zombies that eat the still-warm brains of their victims," Lowry's dad said. "And nowadays that's not what people look for in a package holiday."

"Actually, Dad, she didn't come here for advice," Lowry said. "She wants to borrow one of my dresses so she can look like an A-list celebrity."

"Well, you'd better make sure it's a posh dress — the Walnut Whatnot is eye-wateringly fancy."

"Don't worry, Dad," Lowry said. She snapped her fingers. "I have just the outfit."

A Vile Substitution

I T WAS AN ENORMOUS BLUE BALLGOWN WITH puffy sleeves and a lacy collar and pink piping that looked like cords of icing sugar. Lowry had insisted it was her finest dress. Molly suspected that it was, in fact, a costume that Lowry's sister Frances had once worn in a school play, which Lowry had stolen for use on special occasions.

Molly tried to explain that the journalist would be expecting to meet a twelve-year-old history-nerd, not Lady Jane Piffle, but Lowry brushed her objections aside. "Molly, the point is to make an impression. That way, if you mess things up or do a massive burp during lunch, Gordon Lovage won't even remember. He'll just remember that you were wearing a really, really massive ballgown."

But messing things up was not an option. Ditto burping.

Molly had made a promise.

The gown dragged along the pavement as Molly swished to the Walnut Whatnot on North Circuit Street, past newspaper stands and headlines announcing that the inferno in Howlfair Infirmary had merely been a BIG SMOKY JOKE! (*The Gripenny Gazette*), an EXPLOSION OF FUN! (*The Ethelhael Panopticon*) and A BIT OF A BLAST! (*Howlfair Crier*).

The entrance to the Walnut Whatnot was a slim art deco door sandwiched between a creepy flower shop and an estate agent. Above the door, jutting from the wall, was a wooden stand with shelves (that is, a "whatnot"), with odd fandangles on each shelf. Above this was a round window, behind which, on the first floor, was the restaurant.

Mayor de Ville was standing by the door, and Molly knew instantly from his expression that something was very wrong.

The mayor looked up and blinked several times at Molly's ballgown.

"Mayor de Ville? Are you OK?"

"Molly, the editor of *Country Wonders* called this morning," said the mayor. "Gordon Lovage, the journalist they'd planned to send, is missing."

"Missing?"

"The editor was very apologetic."

Molly's fears — for her mum, for the future of the guesthouse — made her innards lurch. "But ... they need to find him."

"They've tried."

"But we can't let this opportunity slip away, Mr Mayor!"

"I know, Molly, but —"

"Howlfair needs this! The Excelsior Guesthouse needs this!"

"Molly, please be calm. Mr Lovage —"

"Gordon Lovage is the best journalist at *Country Wonders* magazine! Not like those vile Corches siblings, who always make fun of the places they stay, and ... Mr Mayor, why are you looking at me like that?"

Actually, the mayor wasn't looking *at* Molly. He was looking *past* her, his eyes full of alarm.

"Two other journalists have come here in Mr Lovage's place," said Mayor de Ville tightly, his eyes indicating somebody standing behind Molly.

Even before Molly turned around, she had a pretty good idea who was behind her.

Cringing, she rotated.

A very tall woman was gazing down on her with the look of a fox who's cornered a juicy hen.

"Hello, Molly."

It was Lucinda Corches, one of the two nastiest journalists in the world. One of the two journalists that Molly had just called *vile*.

"*Uh-oh*," she mumbled.

All the Wild Corcheses

THE ELEGANT, TOOTHY FACE OVERSHADOWING
Molly had been arranged to look benign, except
for one detail: the upper lip was pulled back in so high
a sneer that Molly half expected the woman to whinny
like a horse. The woman's stubby ponytail was tied,
Molly thought, way too tight; it threatened to tear the
hair — resplendently ebony, shiny as freshly spilled
paint — out by the roots.

And, though Molly wasn't in a position to
criticize: what was going on with Lucinda Corches'
dress? Buttoned throttlingly at the collar, hanging to
the ground in heavy folds, the plum-coloured gown
was even showier than Molly's. It resembled various
giant ship's sails sewn together in an overlapping
pattern.

Then there was the woman's shadow. It sprawled
monstrously across the pavement, so lustrous and oily

that one passer-by opted to jump over it rather than walk through it.

"I'm Lucinda Corches from *Country Wonders* magazine," the woman said in a thrilling low voice. She extended a large hand, some of which Molly grabbed hold of. Lucinda Corches shook Molly's hand as though operating a water pump, and gave a trilling, almost zany laugh. "I must confess, I haven't been described as *wild* for rather a long time!"

Molly blinked, confused. "Wild?"

The mayor said, *"Wild?"*

Lucinda Corches plugged a finger into one ear and gave it a wiggle. "My hearing is not what it once was! Didn't I just hear you say to Mayor de Ville that I and my brother are *wild* and that we *have fun* in whatever town we visit?"

"Um, yeah," said Molly. "I believe I did say wild..."

"She definitely said *wild*, ha ha," spluttered the mayor.

Molly couldn't believe how narrowly she'd just dodged disaster. It was bad enough that the poisonous Lucinda Corches and her brother had been sent to write about Howlfair. But if Lucinda Corches had heard Molly call her *vile* — well, a fatally horrible feature in *Country Wonders* would have been guaranteed. And Molly would've been to blame.

"Orson is at our lodgings, reading books about local legends," Lucinda said in her treacly baritone. "The snooty restaurant owner was rather rude to Orson when he telephoned to book a table, and Orson is refusing to dine here on principle. You and I, Molly, shall have to eat his share of lunch. Have you an appetite?"

Molly would have said she could eat a horse, had not Lucinda Corches looked so much like one. Her stomach took the opportunity to growl.

"I'll take that as a yes," said Lucinda. She caught Molly's arm, turned her around, and marched her past the mayor.

"Mayor de Ville, I shall speak to you anon. Molly, let's stuff fancy food into our faces until it sprays out of our noses. I've heard that this place sits at the very peak of Mount Marvellous."

Dizzy with relief, Molly let Lucinda sweep her — virtually carry her — towards the door. She almost didn't notice that although the woman's tone was jovial, her expression, reflected in the glass of the restaurant door before a lacquered-haired usher opened it, was that of a midnight strangler.

The White Worm

"THE SHOCKING TRUTH," LUCINDA SAID IN A low voice, "is that Gordon Lovage was *fired*."

Molly coughed out some soup and had to dab her mouth with her fancy napkin. Around her was the burble of chatter and of small fountains set in free-standing water features, and the tuning-fork chimes of cutlery. Paintings of aristocrats with bored hooded eyes and bored bloodhounds. Hanging baskets letting down the green Rapunzel locks of fantastical flora.

Lucinda had chosen a window seat. Through the first-floor window, Molly had a godlike view of the street below and its traffic, human and mechanical, looking faraway and alien.

She said: "Fired?"

"This is just between you and me, of course. Your mayor — who has the personality of a disposable air freshener — has no idea. I do not wish him to know."

As she spoke, Lucinda reached into her handbag and withdrew a small gem-studded jewellery box. She placed it beside her cutlery.

"Um, course," said Molly, parking her spoon in her bowl. "Poor Mr Lovage! What happened?"

Lucinda Corches raised a hand and fluttered its long fingers. Molly noticed that the nails were painted black and bore tiny moons in different phases. A waiter appeared. Lucinda made some more fluttery gestures. The waiter bowed and scuttled off, returning with sparkling cucumber water.

"He got *caught*, dear."

"Caught! Doing what?"

"Taking bribes."

Molly gasped. "From who?"

"From everyone!" Lucinda Corches gave one of her hysterical laughs, throwing back her head and opening her eyes wide. "You don't think old Lovey Lovage actually liked those cutesy towns he was forced to visit, do you?"

"Actually, I did," said Molly. "How ... disappointing."

"Horrible, isn't it?" Lucinda drew back her lip and gave Molly a horsey smile. "Being lied to, I mean."

The waiter wafted over to whisk away the bowls and to take orders for the next course.

"My guest will have the carpaccio," Lucinda said in

her heavy, gorgeous voice. "I will have the artichoke and vile rocket salad."

Molly frowned. *Vile rocket?*

The waiter frowned. "Vile rocket, madame?"

Lucinda turned her dark eyes towards Molly while continuing to address the waiter. "My dear boy, I'm sure I said *wild* rocket. But the two words do sound similar — don't they, Molly?"

The waiter babbled apologies and backed away, bowing. Molly squirmed.

Lucinda knew. She knew that Molly had called her *vile*.

"Miss Corches..."

Lucinda held up a hand to shut her up. "Molly, let me tell you something."

"Um, OK."

"Your mayor informs me that you are a keen historian and a researcher of local mysteries. Certain other people I've questioned have added that you are a snoop who enjoys digging up local people's secrets. And I have learned today that you are a liar who calls people *vile* and then denies it to their faces."

"Miss Corches, I didn't mean that you and your brother are vile," Molly said. "I meant that, um, your articles..."

"I have no need of a snooping historian or

a slanderous liar, Molly Thompson," Lucinda interrupted. "Once our meal is finished, I hope not to see you again. My brother and I will write a suitably vile — which is to say, *honest* — feature on this appalling creepy ghost-town without your assistance, then get out of here as fast as our vile legs can carry us."

Other diners were looking over.

"Look, I'm sorry!" said Molly, knocking over her cucumber water. "Miss Corches, I'm really sorry about what I said. It's just that the features I've read in *Country Wonders*..."

"Has it occurred to you that our *vile* features were written with good intentions?"

Molly said, "Huh?"

Lucinda leaned forward. Her shadow fell over Molly. "There are plenty of towns that want to be overrun by tourists. But there are also towns that want to make sure they *don't* get overrun by tourists. People from such towns often *beg* Orson and me to come and write a damning appraisal of their locality — to curb the tidal wave of visitors. And we certainly do *not* accept bribes in return for our services. Too much tourism can ruin a town, Molly..."

Lucinda rocked back in her chair and laughed raucously, eyes rolling in her head, teeth gnashing with each guffaw. The whole restaurant watched.

"Of course," Lucinda cried, "there's not much chance of tourism ruining *this* town!"

The terrified waiter approached with the next courses and set them down. Lucinda dismissed him with a flutter of her night-sky fingernails.

"So you see, Molly — I am not the monster you make me out to be," said Lucinda. "Although if a person upsets me, I have been known to take it very personally. Take the proprietor of this establishment, for example. Orson may have refused to come here today on account of the owner being rude to him on the telephone — but I *never* miss a chance to settle a score."

Lucinda smirked and prised open the little jewellery box that had been waiting beside her fork.

Inside it was a squirming white worm.

She lifted it and dropped it onto her artichoke salad, then shut the box and began to scream.

Molly watched agog as her fellow diners began leaping to their feet. Waiters dropped plates. The poor soul who'd been attending to Molly's table flew over with a face full of terror.

"A worm!" Lucinda Corches shouted, rising. "A worm in my salad!"

Diners gasped and checked their own salads. One man spat a mouthful of food over his boss. A waiter fell into a fountain.

"I am not paying a penny for this poison!" Lucinda snarled, turning on the waiter with raised claws. "I will see this establishment shut down, do you hear me? *Shut down!*"

Lucinda scooped up her jewellery box and dropped it into her handbag, gave Molly a wink, and steamed through the throng of weeping waiters while the other diners waved their hands and shouted for the bill.

Molly sat stunned, watching Lucinda Corches push a waiter away from the doorway to the stairs and descend from view. The restaurant owner emerged frantically from the kitchen and fell over a woman who'd stooped to pick up her coat. Molly heard Lucinda burst onto the street below.

There was no way that Molly could let this horrid woman ruin her town. She'd solemnly promised her mum that she'd rescue the Excelsior. But what could she do?

"Hey!" Molly shouted as she tumbled onto the street and wobbled after the journalist. "Stop!"

At last Lucinda Corches halted outside Belmont's Jewellers. She turned, making a vortex of her plum dress as Molly raced up the street.

"If you're planning on begging me to change my mind," Lucinda said as the girl stepped onto her glossy shadow, "I'll warn you that I despise a groveller."

"I'm not here to grovel," Molly snapped, catching her breath. She stood up straight and looked Lucinda in the eye. The woman seemed a little surprised. "I'm here to say that if you mess with my town, you'll regret it."

Lucinda looked delighted. "Why's that?"

"Because…" Molly wasn't sure. "Because I secretly filmed that trick you pulled in the restaurant with the worm!"

"No you didn't."

"OK, no, I didn't! But I'm going to tell everyone what you did. And I'll tell the mayor that thing you told me not to tell him about Gordon Lovage."

"Fine. Do that. Anything else?"

Molly chewed her lip. "Yes! Lots else!"

"Like what?"

"I'll think of something!" Molly snapped. "I've stood up to *far* scarier bullies than you, Miss Corches."

"Really?"

"Really! And by the way — you *are* vile. Anyone who'd plant a worm in a salad and threaten to ruin a twelve-year-old girl's life is the very summit of Mount Vile! So before you go around getting all upset

116

about being called 'vile', you should take a look in the mirror."

Lucinda smirked. Her ponytail stretched her face, amplifying her dark delighted eyes. Molly took a step back, away from the bite of Lucinda's smirk and the puddle of Lucinda's shadow.

"A stubborn seeker of secret knowledge," the journalist purred at last. "A slave of her own curiosity. A meddling bookworm drawn fatally to the strange. Shy! Nervous! Clumsy!" Lucinda laughed, but it was gentle, rippling. "That's how the people of this town describe you." She narrowed her dark eyes. "But you are the opposite of those things. You are a feisty little tearaway who acts before she thinks."

"I am?"

"My brother and I might have a use for a feisty little tearaway during our stay here," Lucinda Corches said. "I will speak to Orson, and if he is in agreement, we will visit you tomorrow. It's currently half-term, yes?"

Confused, Molly nodded. "Yeah…"

"Listen to me, small feisty tearaway. If we choose to make use of you, you'll get your glowing article in *Country Wonders*. We'll put your dank town on the map. I'll make your dreams come true. But in return, you can forget about enjoying your half-term holidays. You can forget about your friends. You can forget about your family. For the week of our visit — one week, that's all — you will be *ours*, Molly Thompson, body and soul, and you will do whatever we ask." She leaned forward. Her shadow seemed to grow. "Is that understood?"

Molly noticed for the first time that Lucinda's eyes were the colour of aubergines. "Understood."

"Then I will visit soon."

"I live at the Excelsior Guesthouse," Molly blurted. "Down Cecily Craven…"

"I know where you live, Molly Thompson."

With a fluttery wave of her moon-phase fingernails, Lucinda Corches turned, her plum dress hoisting centrifugally, and she sailed away, like a pirate ship leaving harbour.

Just then the tolling of Old Mercy — the big bell that hangs in Howlfair's Dance Square — planted its stamp on the valley air. The sky swelled with the northward flow of crows.

From a few streets away came the sound of a police siren. Usually Molly would have stopped to calculate the police car's distance from her, its direction, where in town it was heading. She might have dashed off to find it, bound by her need to know everything that was going on in Howlfair. She might even have managed to arrive at Longmorrow Lane in time to see two police cars pull up outside Wetherill's Weaponry Store.

Instead, she hurried home, her head full of Lucinda Corches' portentous words.

Forget about your friends. Forget about your family. You will be ours, Molly Thompson, body and soul.

The Lioness of the Thompson Tribe

THERE WAS A SEVENTY-TWO-YEAR-OLD woman in a skull-and-crossbones headband arm-wrestling in the lounge.

She appeared to be losing. Her violet hairdo was wobbling like a jelly on a tumble dryer. She was heaving all her strength against the concrete arm of Mr Kmiecik, whose friends called him "Meech" because when you asked him how to pronounce his surname, he'd sing "Ker-MEEEEECH-ick!"

As Gran's strength gave out, Meech gently, almost kindly, pushed her arm to the table as though pressing the lever on an old-fashioned machine. Molly half expected to see steam hiss from the woman's ears.

"Dang it, Meech!" shouted the woman, waving Molly over with the defeated hand. "Couldn't you have let me win in front of my girl?"

Meech said: "A gentleman does not *let* a lady win."

The lady in question was Molly's paternal grandmother. "Dear God, what are you wearing?" Gran asked Molly. "You look like a … thing on a … cake."

"Lowry lent it to me," said Molly, kissing Gran's candyfloss hair. "What are you doing here, Gran? And why are you arm-wrestling Mr Kmiecik?"

"Your grandmother asked if I was strong enough to help move furniture," Meech explained, "and I said I was an arm-wrestling champion once." He shrugged. "She took it as a challenge."

"I've been drinking these lately," said Gran, holding up a metallic pink plastic bottle bearing the name of an energy drink and a picture of the earth exploding. "My doctor doesn't approve, but I find they make me temporarily as strong as a mountain goat."

"Gran, you can't be drinking energy drinks!"

"Why not? I like energy and I like drinks and I like combining things that I like, so what's not to like?"

Molly held up the bottle. "I just don't think you should be drinking something with the slogan *BANNED IN SWEDEN*. And why are you asking Mr Kmiecik about moving furniture?"

"Because Mrs Considene's selling my flat."

"What!"

"If I move out now she'll pay me a sweet bonus on top of my deposit, and then I can give the money to..." — she tapped her nose — "...to someone who needs it for an emergency." Obviously she was talking about Molly's mum and the unpaid bills. "So I'm moving into the Excelsior Guesthouse! We can spend lots of time together talking about boys and politics."

Molly felt a pulse of panic. She wouldn't have much time to spend with Gran if she was assisting Lucinda Corches for the next week in return for a favourable write-up in *Country Wonders* magazine. And she was pretty sure that Gran wouldn't tolerate a bully like Lucinda Corches ordering her granddaughter around. Gran was the lioness of the Thompson tribe. She'd been thrown out of Neighbourhood Watch for suggesting they hunt criminals with spears. She would eat Lucinda alive, even if she needed a bathtub full of pink energy drink to keep her strength up.

"Boys and politics." Molly smiled feebly. "Sounds good." Gran squinted. "Something's bothering you."

"I'm just thinking about, um, a book I was reading..."

Gran squinted harder. "I can tell when you're fibbing, Molly, so you'd might as well spit it out. Did something happen at that posh lunch your Mum told me about? With Mr Lovely from *Country Blunders*?"

Meech was spectating with baffled amusement.

"Mr *Lovage*," said Molly. "Like the herb. And it's *Country Wonders*. And it turned out that the magazine has sent us a different journalist."

A sudden clang of dropped cutlery made everyone jump. Molly turned to see Mum in the doorway.

"A different journalist?" she spluttered, kneeling to pick up the cutlery. "Who?"

"It's someone called Lucinda, Mum," Molly said. "Gordon Lovage is ill or something, so Lucinda and her brother Orson ..."

Gran snorted. "Orson?"

"... are here instead. They're not as nice as Mr Lovage, but I think they'll still write a good article about Howlfair..."

"And they'll be staying at the Excelsior?" Mum said. "By the way, what on earth are you wearing?"

Molly reddened. "It's Lowry's. And I'm not sure where they'll be staying yet. But Lucinda's going to call round soon to tell me her plans, and I'll try to convince her to move in."

"And what if she says no?"

"Mum, everything'll be fine," Molly sighed, heading towards the door. "Can we talk about this at dinner? I'm feeling very weird in this dress."

"Molly, are you sure that everything's OK with

these new journalists?" Mum said as Molly squeezed past her. "Do you promise?"

Molly spotted Gabriel in the lobby, watching her from beside the guest book, tail swishing. "Promise."

"You are right," Molly heard Mr Kmiecik stage whisper to Gran. "She is lying through her teeth."

A Good Scuffle

AFTER AN EARLY DINNER, MOLLY SAT WITH Mum and Gran drinking hot chocolate in front of the fire.

"Odd being back here in the Excelsior," Gran said, ignoring Mum's gestures alerting her that she had whipped cream on her upper lip. "I'd forgotten old Mrs Hellastroom still lives here. Ah, she was a beauty in her day! A real fashion plate. Lustrous hair like a mermaid's." She sighed. "And look at her now. Face like a burst dinghy."

"Gran, stop being nasty," said Molly.

"Speaking of nasty," said Gran, "these journalists of yours sound like creeps. Creeps from Hell."

"I can handle them," said Molly.

Gran snorted. "That's what your dad always said when he was being bullied at school: *I can handle them.*"

"And he *did* handle them," said Molly defensively. "Sometimes."

"He made the bullies laugh," Mum said, staring at the fire. "It's hard to bully someone when they give you the giggles."

"Great," said Gran. "There you go, Molly — just give 'em the giggles."

"Your dad prevented a fist fight once," said Mum, now wearing the slightly dazed look she always wore when memories overcame her. "It was in the local papers."

Molly looked up mid-sip. "What?"

Mum nodded. "Some people started arguing in the under-fives toy department in Ablemarch's," she told Molly, "and suddenly a fight broke out."

"Wish I'd been there," said Gran. "I enjoy a good department store scuffle."

"Your dad ran over and calmed things down," Mum said. "Everyone thought he was a hero."

"What did Dad say? To calm everyone down?"

"No idea," shrugged Mum. "None of the people involved seemed to remember what he said. And whenever I asked your dad, he just shrugged and made up something silly."

"Sounds about right," said Gran.

Another thoughtful spell of silence.

"I'm off to do some homework," said Molly at last, rising and plucking her mug from the table. "I'll probably get an early night tonight, seeing as I've got to be up by six."

Gran choked on her chocolate. "Six?"

Mum gave Molly a look which said: *Don't tell Gran that Banderfrith has got you cleaning his room. Because she'll strangle him.*

"Um, I'm helping to tidy rooms," said Molly. "Just until Mum can afford, you know, paid staff."

"Why do I get the feeling everyone's keeping secrets from me?" Gran grumbled. "For all I know, these journalists you've invited to live here are serial killers who enjoy murdering old ladies."

Molly felt her face heating up. She didn't think the Corches would turn out to be murderers; but Lucinda Corches was pretty frightful, and she wasn't hopeful that Orson Corches would be any nicer.

What kind of people might be coming to live in the Excelsior Guesthouse?

She was about to find out.

From Between the Graves

MOLLY WAS READING IN HER ROOM WHEN Gabriel launched himself onto her desk, knocking over a small vase and scattering the feathers Molly had poked decoratively into it.

"Gabriel! What are you doing, you dingbat?"

The little cat scratched at the windowpane. Molly went over. Leaning against the desk, she put her face to the glass and stared down into Howlfair New Cemetery.

"What is it?"

She scanned the darkening citadel of mossy crooked tombstones, the scrubby rugs of reindeer lichen, the creeping phlox.

She choked on a rising breath.

A man was sitting on one of the gravestones, looking up at her.

For a moment Molly wondered fantastically if he'd

crawled from a grave — for although a healthily broad frame filled his old-fashioned tweed waistcoat, his face wore the deep, dark hollows of the definitely dead. The eyebrows fanned like playing cards. His bracken hair was void of vitality, its dull brown decaying to grey. It flowed backwards over his head, giving him the look of someone walking into the wind. Even from a distance you could see that his skin was a sickly colour, almost green. He was handsome, but he looked deceased.

Molly realized that he was Orson Corches. She jerked back from the window.

"Holy skunks, Gabriel — he's actually turned up," she said. "This is it. He's come to tell me what he and Lucinda want me to do."

Gabriel scratched at the window.

"It's OK." Molly stroked the cat's tense flank. "He's not a vampire. He's a journalist."

The cat grumbled.

"Gabriel, don't be impolite," said Molly. "It's not the same thing at all."

Then Molly saw Lucinda Corches, down in the graveyard, stepping out from behind a dead cherry tree, swigging from a small bottle. She looked up suddenly and waved at Molly, showed her splendid teeth, then beckoned.

Gabriel hissed.

"Complain all you want," said Molly, "I have to go and meet them. They're going to help save the Excelsior. And stop it with the *Why are they waiting for you in the graveyard?* look."

Gabriel glared down at the graveyard.

"Actually, it's a pretty good question," Molly mumbled, heading for the door. "Keep an eye on me, Gabriel. And wish me luck."

The Silentman

MOLLY WENT THROUGH THE DOOR AT THE back of the kitchen, round the side of the Excelsior, and through the iron gate onto the narrow lane that led to Howlfair New Cemetery. Then through the cobwebby wooden gate whose hinges whinged. Then between the rows of graves, a carousel of crows circling above. The evening was mellow and the sky was carpeted with cloud. The trees pulsed with the complicated songs of robins.

Lucinda Corches came towards Molly with her hands out and her gown — green, high-buttoned — dragging across the grass. Her shadow slid slickly over the graves. One hand still held the bottle.

"Molly Thompson! We would have come to the guesthouse, but my brother spied this marvellous graveyard and wished to soak up the atmosphere. Come and meet him."

Before Molly could move, Lucinda leaned towards her and took her arm and whispered in her ear.

"Tread carefully with Orson. *He's very, very sensitive.*"

Up close, Orson Corches looked less like a skeleton and more like a devil.

Shadows slept in the hollows of his face like spent sailors in hammocks. He was perched, glaring, on the gravestone.

"Orson," said Lucinda, "I'd like you to meet…"

"Not working!" Orson Corches interrupted. He had a voice like an engine in a museum coming unexpectedly to life.

Molly said, "Pardon?"

"Potion's not working," he rumbled at Lucinda. He opened a hand, revealing a small bottle in his palm. He threw it aside. "Not bloody working at all. I'm too old."

Lucinda sighed. "Orson, that's what Molly's here for. Shall I tell Molly about our special project?" She turned to Molly. "I have a secret to share with you."

"A secret?"

"All the time we've been working for *Country Wonders* magazine, my brother and I have been conducting an investigation. Haven't we, Orson?"

Orson shrugged and kicked some soil with a boot.

"It started many years ago, in a Cornish village," Lucinda went on. "Our parents encountered some small children playing a rather scary game, and they asked the locals to tell them the story behind it. They were folklorists, our parents — rather famous in their field — and archaeologists, seekers of legendary treasures. The story they heard from the locals fascinated them." She tilted her head. "Do you ever find yourself obsessed with certain stories, Molly?"

Molly could not remember ever not being obsessed with some story or other. "Um, you could say that."

"Well, our parents became obsessed with the story they heard. Unfortunately, they died before they could finish tracing its origins. When we were old enough, Orson and I picked up where they left off. We began researching that dark legend, and we too became intoxicated by it. We've been tracing its history across the country, from town to town, solving all manner of puzzles and riddles, seeking the story's roots. Sometimes we've persuaded *Country Wonders* to send us to towns pertinent to our investigations. Looking for the wellspring of the legend."

Molly scratched her head. "Um, the legend of…"

"The Silentman," Orson Corches growled.

Lucinda smiled. "The legend of the Silentman, Molly. The legend of a phantom — and of a man who became a phantom. A legend which — we finally discovered — started right here in your town! Our long, painful search for the origin of the story has brought us to Howlfair, and at last we will set eyes on the prize our parents spent years searching for."

Molly looked at Orson, hunched like a vulture. Then back at Lucinda. "The prize?"

"The secret tomb of the man who became the Silentman," said Lucinda. "We want you to help us find it."

Voiceless

"CULTURAL REFERENCES TO A GHOST CALLED the Silentman are surprisingly widespread," Lucinda went on. "In obscure little towns and villages across the country, one finds playground games, sayings, songs, stories — even spells and recipes — about a phantom town crier who rings a flaming bell and has a metal plate over his mouth…"

Upon his gravestone, Orson sniffed loudly.

"Wrongly executed by a corrupt mayor, the phantom — the Silentman — takes revenge by terrorizing townsfolk," said Lucinda. "He …"

"… roams lanes at night," Orson interrupted, "and taps on windows, and turns to smoke and squeezes through keyholes, and floats down chimneys, seeking victims to get his cold hands on."

Suddenly Orson hoisted himself from his gravestone. Molly watched with alarm as he stretched out his hands and began shuffling towards her.

"Orson, don't be silly," Lucinda hissed.

Still he came forward. Molly found herself thinking of the way the ghouls had lurched at her through the dusty stale air of the Loonchance Manor crypts that summer. Her heart began to accelerate. She took a step backwards.

Orson grinned, enjoying her discomfort.

"Whatever you do, don't let the Silentman grab you," Orson said in his tar-smoke tone, still walking towards Molly, his hands grasping. "'Cause if you do, you'll straightaway hear, inside your skull, the deafening scream, the nightmarish roar of rage and betrayal that eternally wails in his rotten soul. Doomed for all time to never let his scream out, silenced by the metal plate fixed over his mouth, he forces his scream into the minds of his victims..."

"That's enough, Orson," Lucinda barked.

Panic was seizing Molly. For some reason, her mind locked onto the memory of Carl Grobman grabbing her in the entrance hall of Loonchance Manor; the memory of that moment when she'd realized that the boy she'd thought was her friend had lured her into a trap. She continued to stumble backwards. She bumped into a tall gravestone and cried out, and suddenly Orson was upon her, his grey grin gaping like an earthquake fissure, and though Molly tried to evade him, he managed to grip her shoulder with a rough palm, just like Carl had gripped her before handing her over to Benton Furlock; then Orson Corches lowered his shadowy face to Molly's ear and let out a raspy, quivering impression of the Silentman's scream.

Weak, legs wobbling, Molly squirmed free and stumbled around the gravestone, putting it between her and the journalist.

"*Manners*, Orson!" Lucinda called.

Orson stood up. The dark eye sockets glowered triumphantly. "Then the Silentman drifts away," he hissed, "leaving you standing frozen, petrified. Motionless. Voiceless. To outsiders you appear strangely calm..." He tapped his skull. "But inside your head, that ceaseless shriek goes on and on. The scream of betrayal. It consumes your consciousness. Devours your sanity. Till you wither. Till you die."

"OK, got it," Molly said, trying to keep the shakes from her voice.

"Obviously, we didn't come to Howlfair to look for a murderous phantom," said Lucinda. "The Silentman was once a real person. We believe his tomb is here in the Ethelhael Valley — and that our parents were searching for it when they ... when we were younger.

For years Orson and I have striven to discover what our parents expected to find in that tomb, and why they went to such lengths to locate it. Did they simply wish to come face to face with the legendary figure who had fascinated them for so long? Or were they searching for some precious artefact?"

"*The flaming bell*," said Orson. Briefly Molly saw his eyes flash within their recesses. "The fiery bell with the power to banish ghosts and summon Hell."

"Indeed," said Lucinda. "There may be a bell of enormous power — or at least enormous value — buried in the town crier's secret tomb. But we haven't found any records that might tell us exactly *where* he's buried. That's where you come in."

A Harmless Potion

MOLLY'S LEGS WERE STILL QUAKING. SHE thought she could hear the Silentman's scream of betrayal, but it was just the rushing of blood behind her temples.

"So you want me to help you … find his remains?"

"Oh, get rid of her," Orson growled at his sister. "You can see she's a quivering coward. One sip of the potion would send her doolally."

"Beg pardon?" Molly said, frowning.

"Orson, I'm sure Molly will be fine with drinking the potion," Lucinda said.

Molly leaned against the crumbling cross of the tombstone. "What … potion?"

"A harmless herbal potion that makes one sensitive to the traces left by the past," Lucinda expanded. "Orson believes it lets one hear the voices of the dead. I — being a rationalist — believe it enables one to detect the electromagnetic imprints that historical events leave on the atmosphere. You'll need to drink it if you're going to be of use to us."

"It gives you ears to hear the voices of the tormented dead," Orson said. "If you got the guts to hear 'em."

"That's another way of putting it." Lucinda held up the bottle and examined the purple liquid. "We came across the potion years ago, in a village in Herefordshire famous for its witches. Marvellous stuff — but it works better on the young. It has very little effect on me these days — and virtually no effect at all on my brother. Which is why we need someone young and innocent to drink it, to help us locate the Silentman's grave. To complete our parents' mission to discover the source of the Silentman story." She held out the bottle. "Want to try a sip?"

What madness was this? Surely, Molly thought, Lucinda didn't expect a twelve-year-old girl to drink some weird herbal concoction that might send her doolally?

With a lurch of guilt, Molly remembered that she had given Lowry a weird herbal concoction that very summer, an anti-lycanthropy potion which she'd made herself, using a recipe she'd found in the 1612 edition of Follington's *Botanicals*. Lowry had ended up in hospital, poisoned.

What if Molly were allergic to the Corcheses' potion and ended up in Howlfair Infirmary? She wouldn't be much use to anyone there. And as for hearing the voices of the tormented dead — no thanks. And also: she was *Molly Thompson*. The best twelve-year-old historian in the valley, and probably in the country, and perhaps in the universe. If she couldn't find a secret grave using brainpower alone, she might as well give up investigating historical mysteries and take up badminton.

"I'll pass, thanks," she said. "I prefer to solve mysteries with … you know, my brain."

"See!" Orson barked. "A coward! Worse than a coward — a coward who thinks she's clever." He let out a sigh that was also a growl. "I'm off," he said, cricking his neck loudly. "This was a waste of time."

Then he strode away, crunching over twigs, aiming for the gathering of tall trees to the north-east of the graveyard.

Molly saw her chances of rescuing the Excelsior, of rescuing Howlfair, of keeping her promise to Mum, evaporating.

And suddenly she was running after Orson, through the graveyard, tripping over shrubs, her desperation overpowering her fear.

"Wait!"

Wits Alone

AS MOLLY NEARED HIM, AT THE GRAVEYARD'S perimeter, Orson stopped and span, as though hoping to scare her again. But this time she steeled herself. She walked right up to him. No matter how scary Orson Corches was, he surely wasn't as scary as the prospect of telling Mum that she'd bungled her chance to save the guesthouse.

She stepped into his shadow and glared up into the hollows of his face.

"You listen to me," she said, as sternly as she was able. "I don't need a stupid potion to find a grave."

Orson looked disdainful. "Is that right?"

Molly put her hands on her hips. It seemed appropriate. "I've never failed to solve a historical mystery in this town," she said. "Finding a hidden grave is the kind of thing I do before breakfast."

Orson raised a hedge-like eyebrow. He opened his

mouth to speak, but Molly cut him off.

"John Broome," she said.

At the mention of the name, Lucinda and Orson exchanged a look of surprise.

"What do you know of Broome?" Orson rumbled.

"He was Howlfair's town crier between 1711 and 1738," said Molly, "back in the Dark Days, when Howlfair was supposedly full of ghosts and monsters. He was famous for his booming voice, which you could hear for miles. Every day Broome rang his town crier's bell in the Dance Square and shouted 'Hear ye, hear ye!' and read out notices, and he used to ring Old Mercy — which is the big bell in the square — to warn when ghosts or monsters were sighted..."

By now Lucinda had joined them. The sky had leaked its light and the crows were calling out like market sellers.

"Go on," Lucinda said.

"John Broome was a hero," Molly said. "He'd plead the cause of the poor and the helpless in his daily announcements, and he'd criticize the mayor, who was lazy and corrupt. The townsfolk loved him. The mayor hated him. Then John Broome saved Howlfair from a gang of angry ghosts — he used his bell — he'd had it blessed by the priest of St Fell's in a special ceremony — to lead the ghosts out of town, and he locked them in a secret vault and refused to give away its location."

"I told you the girl knew her fables, Orson," smirked Lucinda.

Molly went on. "The corrupt mayor was jealous of Broome's popularity, and furious that Broome was always challenging his authority. So, taking advice from a nasty friend of his — a bishop from a nearby county — the mayor made false accusations, and convinced the townsfolk that Broome had been to blame for the invasion of phantoms in the first place — that he'd used his bell to *summon* them. A jeering crowd watched as their former hero was publicly hanged with a metal plate over his mouth and the bell tied to his hand. He was buried in a secret location, along with his victims, whose bodies were considered cursed. According to the legend, he was buried still holding the bell, which nobody could prise out of his grip."

"The bell..." Orson muttered dreamily.

Molly went on. "After that — according to the story — Broome's phantom began haunting the town. His touch drove people insane. The whole town was in a panic. The mayor promised to deal with the phantom, and he got help from his friend the bishop, who came to Howlfair and trapped the ghost in a snuffbox — the traditional way of trapping ghosts — and threw the box into the Six Bridges Stream." She turned back to Orson. "John Broome is the man who became the Silentman. It's his tomb you've been looking for."

Lucinda said, "We already know this story, Molly Thompson. But how do you know it?"

"My dad told it to me," she said. "He died a few years ago, but John Broome was one of his heroes. Dad said that John Broome gave a voice to voiceless people. He spoke up for people who never usually got listened to. That's why the mayor stuck a metal plate over Broome's mouth before executing him — to mock him. To silence him."

"Your father sounds like he was an interesting man," said Lucinda.

"Yeah, he was," said Molly. She turned to Orson. "And if he'd heard you speaking to me the way you just did, he would've knocked you out."

Orson grimaced. The wind grew in force as the evening darkness fell. The shadowy trees around the graveyard all did the same horrible dance.

"Orson and I understand what it means to lose parents too soon," Lucinda said. "Our parents vanished during their investigations. We're hoping that if we find the secret resting place of John Broome,

145

we might find clues about what happened to our parents." She clasped her big hands. "You can imagine how hard it is, can't you? To not know what happened to a loved one?"

Molly didn't need to imagine. Her dad had died of a heart attack after a sudden and (Molly thought) mysterious illness. Benton Furlock — before Molly had banished him — had claimed to know secrets about the circumstances surrounding Dad's death. But since overcoming Furlock's ghouls, Molly had been trying hard to obsess less about her dad's death. If her only route to the truth was through the hideous Benton Furlock, then she would rather leave the truth alone. At least for now.

"My dad wouldn't want me drinking some weird potion," she said, moving away from Orson. "He taught me that there's no mystery I can't solve if I use my brain."

"And what if finding Broome's grave is the one mystery this brain of yours can't solve?" Orson said gruffly. "What if there are no clues to be found?"

"There are *always* clues," said Molly. "Nobody ever hides anything without leaving traces. The truth always finds a way of leaking out. Back in the Dark Days, people who hid things often left clues on purpose, just in case future generations needed to find the things they'd hidden. I know how to uncover secrets, Mr Corches. Because as far as I'm concerned, there's no such thing as a secret, not really."

"Orson, why don't we give Molly a chance?" said Lucinda. "If, over the next week, it transpires that Molly can't find Broome's grave using her wits alone, *then* she'll use our potion." She smiled sweetly at Molly. "That strikes me as an acceptable compromise — yes? Especially since you're so adamant that you'll easily find the grave without any herbal help." She drew near and held out a hand. "Do we have a deal?"

Molly didn't want to say yes.

She distrusted the Corcheses. And she distrusted the Corcheses' creepy potion.

She had no desire to hear the voices of the tormented dead.

But too much was at stake. She needed the Corcheses' help to save the Excelsior from ruin. Anyway, as long as she could find the grave of John Broome, she wouldn't have to take the potion, would she?

How hard could it be to find a flipping grave?

She took Lucinda's hand. "Deal."

"Excellent!" Lucinda cried, breaking away. "We will make arrangements with your mayor to have the Excelsior prepared, and we will move our things from our current lodgings."

Orson sulked.

"Um, did you say you'd have the Excelsior prepared?" Molly said.

"The mayor will contact your mother tonight. We'll get our M&R team over to Howlfair immediately."

The crows careened. "M&R team?"

"Makeovers and Renovations. Your mayor has already agreed to pay for everything we need during our stay. If you help us find the grave our parents were searching for — with or without the aid of our potion — we'll turn your guesthouse into the Ritz and Howlfair into the Marina di Portofino. On one condition."

Molly didn't know what the Marina di Portofino was, but that seemed beside the point. "What condition?"

"As far as anyone's concerned, you are merely our tour guide. The Silentman is to be our secret. Understood?"

Molly nodded.

"Good," said Lucinda, taking Orson's arm to lead him away as straggles of mist sniffed their way across the graveyard. "Because if you tell a soul about our project to find the grave of the Silentman..."

Orson concluded the sentence. "We will make your life hell."

Suddenly Orson gasped. At that moment, a meow cut through the air.

148

Turning, Molly saw Gabriel leap onto a crypt. He was silhouetted against the sky beside a statue of an angel, back arched, fur on end, hissing.

"What's that hairy thing?" Orson cried. "With the teeth?"

"He's Gabriel," said Molly. "My cat."

Lucinda gave Gabriel a look of alarm. "It's not an ordinary cat, is it?"

He wasn't; Molly's gran had once told her that the owners of the Excelsior Guesthouse, throughout the centuries, had always been guarded by mysterious cats. Molly said, "He protects me."

As if to prove her point, the scruffy creature leapt down and galloped over to join Molly. Orson screamed.

"Keep that creature away," Lucinda snarled. "Keep it away from me and my brother, you understand?"

Molly looked at Gabriel. "Um, OK..."

With a whirl of her green dress, Lucinda dragged Orson off. "We move in tomorrow," she called. "And we don't want to see that cat."

Together they fled the graveyard, heading into the belt of trees.

"They must be allergic," said Molly.

Gabriel looked insulted.

"I can tell you don't like the Corcheses, Gabriel," said Molly. "I don't have warm feelings towards them

149

myself. But they're going to be living with us for a week, so you should probably keep your distance. And stop it with the *They remind me of a couple of vampires* look."

Gabriel squinted at the Corches as they disappeared into the woods.

"Yeah, me too," Molly confessed.

Molly lingered in the graveyard, pondering the future, watching as crows flew on crowy errands and the sky went to sleep. She had a feeling that a great change was about to sweep over the Excelsior Guesthouse and over her life and over Howlfair. And eventually she went back indoors, Gabriel at her heels, to find that the change had already begun.

Makeovers and Renovations

MOLLY WAS HEADING THROUGH THE LOBBY when a small cry issued from Mum's office.

"Mum, are you OK?"

As Molly moved towards the office door, she caught her mother's shaky voice:

"Of course! That's ... unbelievable. Thank you. We'll be here, yes."

Then the door opened and Mum lurched forth amidst a mad tangle of hair, her eyes aglow.

"Molly! Molly, you'll... You'll never —"

"Come on, Mum, spit it out."

"The mayor phoned! Those journalists — they want to move into the Excelsior tomorrow! They've asked the mayor to have the place done up, as we'll be featured in *Country Wonders* magazine!"

"Done up — by *tomorrow*?"

"He says that a special makeover squad is on its

way to Howlfair! Plumbing, electrics, interior design, decorating... Molly, it's like a crazy dream — and it's all your doing!"

"But how're they going to get it done by tomorrow?"

Mum shrugged. "No idea," she said. "But they'll be here this evening, so I guess we'll see."

When the M&R team arrived, in six dark vans, it was like an invasion.

There was a hygiene inspector. Three interior designers. A team of gardeners. A landscaping expert. Lots of ladders and vats of paint and machines and clipboards...

"This," Mum whispered to Molly, "is going to cost the mayor a fortune."

A suited woman got Mum to sign various forms (Mum didn't have time to read what she was signing) while the rest of the team swarmed, putting up ladders, measuring, drawing plans, consulting plans.

"Why was I not told of this intrusion?" Banderfrith ranted. "How dare these identical people barge into my home and start painting things!"

Gran and Mum tried to calm him down, but it was hard to pacify Mr Banderfrith when he was annoyed *and* overtired.

"I'm going to bed," he announced in a wobbly voice.

"If these people disturb my sleep, I will leave so fast it will make everybody's head fall off. Everybody's!"

Amazingly, though, once everyone was in bed, Molly included, the people from the A&K RENOVATIONS vans worked in total silence. Molly fell asleep almost as soon as she climbed under her duvet with its *Curse of the Mummy* cover, even though her head was crawling with excited speculations on what kind of guesthouse might greet her in the morning.

Of the Excelsior's residents, only Gabriel had a sleepless night. He sat at Molly's bedroom door with a concerned frown, and occasionally paced back and forth as though preparing for some gathering doom.

The New Excelsior

MOLLY WAS DREAMING THAT SHE WAS ON the bandstand in the Dance Square, standing next to the old stocks. Felicity Quick was floating before her in a grey gown. Around her stood the people of Howlfair.

"I reckon," said Felicity in a voice not her own, "that Molly secretly *wants* the Dark Days to come back."

Molly shook her head and tried to speak, but her breath caught in her throat — for suddenly Felicity began to transform. Her skin became ashen; a jewel-encrusted eye patch slid around her face like a serpent and came to rest over one eye; her hair grew upward, turning grey, and from it many-legged insects began to crawl, and death's head moths.

Lady Orgella, the Mistress of Ghouls.

Molly finally woke up with a yelp. Gabriel was

pawing at her face. Spluttering, she sat up and looked at her alarm clock.

7.08. She was late for Mr Banderfrith's room.

Tripping over her feet, shaking the horrid dream from her mind, she dressed in mad haste and grabbed the spare key from her desk drawer.

Out in the corridor, shoes untied, she hardly had time to notice the changes that had been made overnight. The gleaming white of the walls; the polished porthole windows; the new varnish on the giant timber beams that braced the higgledy corridors. Carpets had been pulled up to expose dark wooden floors, making the Excelsior look even more like a haunted galleon. Creepy oval portraits haunted the walls. Even the fire extinguishers — huge gleamy copper things — looked beautiful (though, frankly, too heavy to lift).

And what'd happened to the spiral staircase? The steps now seemed to be made of jade. Jars — possibly funeral urns — sat in carved alcoves that had not existed only hours before. The stairs were gorgeously lit by glowing antique lanterns. From somewhere, or nowhere, classical music played.

Molly tumbled into Banderfrith's room to find the man standing there with his arms folded and his wig in place, numerous suitcases and boxes packed.

"Late!" he cried. "We had a deal, Thompson — and you broke it! I'm moving out!"

His moustache twitched fearsomely. His eyes and toupée gleamed.

"Well?" Banderfrith roared. "No apology? No grovelling?"

Molly realized that Banderfrith hadn't seen the renovations yet. She stifled a smirk.

"Okey doke, Mr B.," she shrugged, turning to go. "I'll tell Mum you're leaving."

"What!" Banderfrith wailed, clutching his heart. "The effrontery! The calumny! I'll have this place shut down, you curly-topped imp!"

"Fine!" Molly said brightly. She turned in the doorway. "But you might want to see last night's renovations before you take your suitcases downstairs."

Like duelling dodgem cars they bumped into each other as they bumbled down the corridor to the staircase. There Banderfrith stalled, overwhelmed.

Molly surged past him — and caught sight of the lobby...

It was unspeakably marvellous! From the patterned tiles — marble — to the vaulted ceiling with its gigantic chandelier. Stone ravens perched ready to swoop down from the archway that soared over the mouth of the

156

stairwell. And there, beside the desk with the white and gold telephone and the guestbook, stood Molly's mother, mouth open, shaking her head with wonder.

Banderfrith joined Molly. "Dear God!"

"How did they do it?" blurted Molly.

"I have no idea," Banderfrith whispered. They stood and stared.

"So you'll be staying, Mr Banderfrith?" Molly said at last. The old man huffed and tutted.

"I believe I will."

Molly turned to him. "And what about our arrangement?"

Mr Banderfrith frowned sourly and licked his teeth for a while. And at length his face seemed to soften, until it could almost be mistaken for the face of someone about to set a girl free from the burden of cleaning duties. Molly looked hopefully at his changing expression.

It soured once more, and set hard.

"You're on your last warning," he grumbled, heading down the steps. "Now go and clean my room."

Starting Place

IT WASN'T EASY FOR MOLLY TO CLEAN MR Banderfrith's room efficiently while also day-dreaming about throwing him down a well. The job took her the best part of an hour. When Molly returned downstairs, muscles aching, she found Mum talking to Lucinda in the lobby while Orson read a pamphlet by the information stand. Lucinda was wearing a voluminous pink and green exclamation mark of a ballgown, which Mum was struggling not to be distracted by.

"Ah, the lady herself!" Lucinda said, fluttering her moon-phase nails at Molly. "I hope you like the improvements we've made. I was just telling your surprisingly glamorous mother about today's assignment."

Mum blushed. "Why didn't you tell me you were showing Lucinda and Orson around the library this morning?" she asked Molly.

158

"Library?" said Molly, looking at Lucinda. "Must have, um, forgotten…"

"The great Molly Thompson — forgetful?" Lucinda laughed. "Surely not!"

Orson, flicking through a brochure, let out a snort.

Lucinda turned her eyes towards Molly. "Shall we head to the library and put that famous brain of yours to the test?"

Molly didn't like the metallic note of challenge in Lucinda's voice.

Orson opened the front door of the guesthouse to reveal, on the gravel driveway, a luxury saloon car, black and chrome, with a hatted driver. On the door was written, in fancy silver script, a logo: A&K.

"Wow," said Molly, crunching across the gravel.

The driver stepped out and opened the rear door. Lucinda gestured for Molly to get in. Moments later Molly was sitting between the Corches siblings, on a back seat that resembled a leather sofa, surrounded by the treacly purr of the car's engine. Soon they were in motion, the car moving so smoothly down Cecily Craven Street that Molly fancied it was hovering.

Nobody spoke. Orson leafed noisily through a pamphlet about Howlfair Library. "Rubbish," he mumbled at last. "How can a library be mechanical? How can its rooms move?"

Molly said, "They're on pulleys. The Order of Tehuti rebuilt the interior during the Dark Days, because..."

"Actually, we're not interested in your library," said Lucinda, reaching across Molly and snatching the pamphlet. "We're dropping you off so you can start researching the Silentman. We have other things to attend to."

Molly saw the driver smirk into the rear-view mirror. "Um, sorry?"

"The library, Molly — that's where you usually start your investigations, isn't it? You dig your way through old books and records and you fill notebooks with your ideas. Your mother told us all about it."

"You've got till tonight," said Orson.

"Tonight?" coughed Molly, anxiety rising. She rubbed her eyes — it seemed like the outside world was streaking past at an impossible speed. "To what — find where John Broome is buried?"

"To tell us where to start looking," Lucinda said. "Is he likely to have been interred in a graveyard? On private property? Flung into an unmarked grave? I want our investigations to make significant progress every day. Otherwise..."

"Otherwise we do things our way," said Orson. He mimed swigging from a bottle.

"I expect to be impressed, Molly," Lucinda said.

"Silly-looking place," mumbled Orson, leaning against Molly to glare through the windscreen as the car swung around. Molly was surprised to find that they'd already arrived at the library. She looked past Lucinda at the building, built in 1537, with its chubby body made from enormous rocks resembling leftovers from Stonehenge. The place didn't look silly to Molly. Studded with tall flags, it made Molly think of a harpooned but defiant monster. The randomly distributed eye-shaped windows blinked orange with fireplace flames. The oval observatory balanced on top of the bewilderingly tall tower like a wise head on a proud neck. Molly felt her usual thrill at the sight of the building, home to endless corridors and forbidden rooms; but today the thrill was tinged with trepidation.

The car slid into the parking area.

The driver got out and moments later Molly had been released. Lucinda rolled down her window.

"This is your first test," she said. "Let's see if your investigative skills are as good as everyone says they are."

Bossy Old Bag

MOLLY WOULD'VE QUITE LIKED TO HAVE shown the Corches around the library.

If you believed the old stories (and Molly did), Howlfair Library was haunted. It had often been subject to attack by monsters during the Dark Days, the gruesome period in Howlfair's history that began with some early settlers stumbling on a gateway to Hell while mining for priceless oquiel, releasing a sinister mist with supernatural powers. In those days, the library was also often the venue of vicious fighting between Howlfair citizens eager to gain possession of precious books. Would-be warlocks had raided the library, seeking the knowledge to control Howlfair's fiends for their own ends. Glory-hunters had sought clues about how to defeat monsters; crooks had sought to steal books in order to force others to pay for the knowledge they contained.

Molly could have told the Corches siblings about the special group that arose to protect the library: the Order of Tehuti. She would have explained how members of the order rebuilt the insides so that all rooms could be locked centrally to trap troublemakers. Moreover, the rooms could be *moved around*. In an emergency, huge winches would rearrange the library's halls and deliver troublemakers to a special gate at the rear of the library, where law enforcers would be standing ready to arrest them.

But of course Molly didn't get to show the Corcheses around the library, because she'd been dumped here and ordered to find where a wrongly executed town crier was buried. She ambled through reception, trying to disregard the mean glare of Mrs Brank, who disliked Molly for unmentioned reasons.

"Morning, Mrs Brank," she mumbled.

Though always dowdily dressed in grey and brown, Mrs Brank had a fondness for exotic sparkly 1950s spectacles that made her look like a magnified cat. She narrowed her eyes behind the winged red frames.

"*No mischief,*" Mrs Brank hissed. "Got that?"

As if in response, Molly's stomach rumbled noisily.

"And less of your grumbling!" Mrs Brank snapped. "I'm not someone to mess with, Molly Thompson."

"Course not, Mrs Brank," Molly said, adding the words *bossy old bag* under her breath. She peered up at the archways leading to different parts of the library. The flags. The plaques. The pulleys and chains that could whisk the rooms away. She inhaled the lovely grim history, and formulated her plan of attack.

This was her territory. This was where she was at her best.

She pushed up her jumper sleeves. They slipped back down as she walked past the ancient wooden sign that listed various rules of conduct (NO RUNNING — NO RAISED VOICES — NO NECROMANCY...).

"Right, John Broome," she said, cracking her knuckles. "Let's find where your dead bones are buried."

Flipping nothing!

Nothing!

No records of John Broome's burial. No mentions in history books.

In fact, there were no books about John Broome or the Silentman at all — only spaces on shelves where Molly had expected to find books.

She checked with Mrs Brank, who grumpily consulted the catalogues and confirmed that the library *did* stock books about the Silentman story —

and nobody had withdrawn them. Which meant (Molly thought but did not say) they'd been stolen.

Stolen by whom?

The morning evaporated. The afternoon wore on, and all Molly had written in her notepad were the words THE SILENTMAN and a picture of the Silentman. Molly managed to find an interesting-looking volume about secret burial sites — but there was a page missing, torn out, where she'd hoped to find information about Broome's resting place.

Then, as if the disappearance of information about the Silentman wasn't weird enough, Molly saw something even more baffling.

Lockdown

IT WAS A FAMILIAR-LOOKING ELFIN GIRL WITH bobbed golden hair, emerging from the Medical Books room with a stack of tomes and printouts while Molly stood drinking from a paper cup at the water fountain.

"Lowry?"

Lowry shouted "Yipes!" and dropped her books and stooped to scoop them up. "Molly! Why are you here?"

Molly rolled her eyes. "I came to try out these paper cups everyone's talking about," she said, dropping the empty cup into the bin.

"No need to be sarcastic."

"I'm researching something for the Corcheses," Molly said, holding up her notepad. "What are you doing?"

"Also researching!" said Lowry. "Werewolf stuff."

"I thought you'd got over thinking you were a werewolf?"

"Well, can't hurt to do some extra research, can it?" said Lowry, lifting up her books and documents.

"But weren't you banned from the library for a month after our last school visit? For roller skating down the stairs?"

"I sneaked in," Lowry said proudly.

There was a sound of footsteps on stairs. Then Felicity came bowling through a nearby doorway into the corridor, waving a book. "Look! A book about lock picking! Oh — hi, Molly."

Molly was confused. She turned to Lowry. "You came here with Felicity?"

"I needed a lookout," said Lowry. "And I know how much the werewolf thing annoys you. So..."

"So I think we'd better scarper," Felicity butted in. "*Listen.*"

From the stairwell at the corridor's end came the unmistakable sound of Mrs Brank singing a dirge. Molly heard the woman's flat-footed steps on the stairs.

"Run!" hissed Lowry, grabbing Molly's arm.

The girls sprinted down the corridor. Felicity dived through the nearby doorway into the Medieval History room, nearly slipping on the varnished floor; she grabbed a life-sized medieval peasant dressed in a grain sack, part of a huge display made by schoolchildren, in an attempt to regain her balance. The peasant's hat fell onto Lowry's head as she dragged Molly through the doorway.

"Lowry, slow down!"

But now Lowry was slipping on the floorboards. She released Molly and began wheeling her arms, struggling to remain upright. Molly crashed into the peasant, which toppled on her, dragging the rest of the display off its platform. Molly slipped to one knee and thrashed and somehow ended up inside one of the grain sacks, and she blundered after her friends like a haunted scarecrow, waving her arms and spitting out straw.

Felicity collided with a wall. Lowry stumbled into a bookshelf, grabbing a lever on the wall for support. It cranked rustily, and suddenly ancient cogs within the walls started moving—

"What's going on?" Lowry squealed, throwing off her peasant hat, which had fallen over her eyes.

Heavy iron screens slid down over the doorways, locking the girls in the Medieval History room.

"You've activated the lockdown mechanism designed in 1715," gasped Molly. "The one under that massive DO NOT TOUCH sign."

From further down the corridor came the sound of Mrs Brank shouting.

"Why's the room's moving?" Felicity cried.

"The library's like one of those puzzles with sliding pieces," said Molly. "Other rooms are moving out of the way so that this room can be delivered mechanically to the rear of the library, where a group of armed guards would've been waiting. If we were in 1715, that is. Now, though, it's going to be something much worse."

"Mrs Brank!" gasped Lowry as the room lurched upwards. "Oh, we're dead!"

"Why did you have to flipping get me involved?" snapped Molly, throwing off the sack. The room rumbled sideways. Books toppled. "I'm supposed to be doing research for the journalists, and now Mrs Brank will think I came here to get up to mischief with you two."

Ancient pulleys and chains groaned. Screams echoed. Molly heard Mrs Brank barking somewhere. The room juddered and Molly stumbled forward. Lowry fell to the floor and clung to a pamphlet display. Then the room seemed to speed up, and then it turned a corner, rotating. Unseen chains emitted a metallic shriek. A book fell on Lowry's head and she screamed. She picked it up. "Oh, wow, this only ever happens in stories! Look — an ancient book that'll solve all our problems!"

"Really?" said Felicity.

"Yes! See — the wildly thrilling *Medieval Property Law in Howlfair*, seventeenth edition."

"Oh, shut up, Lowry," said Felicity.

The room shivered horribly and stopped. Then the metal screen covering the door nearest Felicity began to rise.

The door opened and the three girls blinked at the sunlight.

Outside, in a walled area once used for the apprehension of dangerous troublemakers and monsters, stood Mrs Brank.

"Well, look who it is," she said, adjusting her cat-eye spectacles as though focusing a camera. "You horrible little toerags are barred. For life."

"What!" cried Molly. "You can't do that!"

"I think you'll find that us bossy old bags can do whatever we like in our own libraries."

Molly winced. The librarian had heard Molly insult her earlier.

Mrs Brank climbed aboard the library, shut the door and eased down the lever on the wall, listening carefully to the clicks as it slotted into various gears. She released it, the iron plates slid down, and once again the Medieval History room was in motion.

"You can leave through the door in my office," Mrs

Brank said as chains clanked and the room shifted. "If you don't want me to tell your parents about your adventure today, make sure I never see you near my library again."

The shamefaced girls were ejected and stood miserably on Brothwell Lane. Molly was in a panic.

"I can't get barred from the library now!" she said as Lowry and Felicity tried to drag her away. "I'm supposed to be doing something! Researching something for the Corcheses!"

Lowry took a book from her pocket and handed it to Molly. "Oh — you dropped this," she said. It was Molly's notepad, open at the first page, on which Molly had written THE SILENTMAN and drawn a picture of the phantom town crier. "Doesn't really look like you were researching something for the Corcheses. I thought the whole idea of you being their tour guide was to show them that Howlfair isn't all scary monsters…"

"It's a secret thing, OK?" Molly blurted, stuffing the notepad into her jeans pocket. "I mean, it's something they're interested in and they want me to investigate it…"

Lowry and Felicity looked at each other.

"I think it's time for a trip to Timbrel's," said Lowry,

steering Molly down the road, away from the off-limits library. "We'll get a booth and have a cream tea and you can tell us all about him."

"Him?" said Felicity.

"This Silentman fellow."

Finding the Dead

"**THEY WANT YOU TO HELP THEM FIND A** grave?" said Lowry through a mouthful of scone. "What's that got to do with writing a feature for Country Wonders?"

They were sitting in their favourite booth in Timbrel's Tea Rooms, under a tin sign advertising

TIMBREL TEAS:
The Fortune-Teller's Choice

CHUJEN ITCHING
POWDER TEA
An Exotic Brew for
Divination and Wisdom.

(The Timbrel Tearooms had once been a famous haunt for tea-leaf readers and other soothsayers.)

"It's just some local history they're interested in," Molly said. "But now I won't be able to do any research because I'm flipping banned from the library." She thought with dread of the Corcheses' ghastly potion. "This evening Lucinda's going to ask me what I've managed to find out, and I'll have to say, 'Well, Lucinda, funny you should ask! I found out absolutely nothing…'"

"'And the library spat me and my friends out,'" added Lowry. "'Actually spat us out.'"

"I don't think you should be looking for some guy's grave," said Felicity. "For all you know, his ghost — the Silentman — is locked inside it along with his remains." She chewed her scone reflectively. "For all you know, the Silentman is the monster in that prophecy you found in that book. The one trapped in some crypt."

"Can't be — a bishop trapped the Silentman in a snuffbox in 1738 and threw the box into the Six Bridges Stream," said Molly.

"A snuffbox?" said Lowry.

"It's an old method for catching ghosts — you do a special ritual and force the ghost to go into a little tin box and then you put the lid on and throw the box into a stream or river."

"So this tomb is just going to contain a skeleton?

The skeleton of John Broome?"

"And maybe a handbell of great historical significance that may also have supernatural powers," said Molly.

"Ah — so basically you're helping these journalists loot someone's grave," said Felicity. "Got it."

"They're not looting, they're investigating," Molly protested. "And Lucinda's going to flip her lid when I tell her I haven't made any progress. She might even fire me and leave the Excelsior and undo all the changes they've made to the place."

"What changes?" said Felicity.

Molly explained.

"Jeepers," said Lowry. "I can see why you'd want to keep them sweet. Your mum must be over the moon."

"I haven't seen her this happy for years," said Molly. "She doesn't know that her happiness depends on me finding the ancient remains of a hanged man."

"My mum would be happy if I just remembered to pick up my socks," said Lowry.

Felicity said, "Why not just ask Grobman to help? He's a gravedigger."

"Not a *real* one," said Molly curtly. "He plays a Victorian gravedigger during ghost tours. There's a difference." In addition to working in Mr Wetherill's shop, Carl Grobman had an evening job with the

175

tourist board. "I wouldn't expect a fake gravedigger to help me find a secret burial site."

"I agree with Molly," said Lowry. "That would be like asking a soap-opera doctor to take your tonsils out."

"Just ask him," said Felicity. "You never know what secrets are lurking under that greasy hair."

"I'd rather eat my own arms than have to trust Carl for something," Molly grumbled.

"Well, you've got a grave to find, and you've been banned from the library," said Felicity. "Seems to me you don't have much choice."

Molly stared unhappily at the table. Someone had carved their initials into it. She thought of how Benton Furlock had branded Carl with the mark of Lady Orgella, Mistress of Ghouls. For all Molly knew, the demon was still planning to use Carl to ensnare her.

My own dear, doomed Molly…

No — she wasn't going to ask Carl. She was never going to trust Carl for anything ever again. Even if she'd have to face the Corcheses that evening and admit that she'd failed her first test.

Even if she ended up having to drink the Corcheses' sinister potion so that the creepy voices of dead people could tell her where to find John Broome's grave.

But she really, *really* hoped it wouldn't come to that.

"Hey, *we* can help you, if you like," said Lowry. "I can subtly ask my dad if he knows anything about secret burial sites. Maybe there are records somewhere in the tourist office. Do you think you'll be able to get your journalists to give you more time?"

"No idea," said Molly. "If Lucinda doesn't bite my head off, her brother probably will."

She drained the tea that Lowry had kindly bought her. It was time to go home and face her doom.

On the way back to Cecily Craven Street, Molly paused outside Ablemarch's Department Store. She peered through the gold-framed glass of the revolving door, past the lobby in which staff lingered over-helpfully in gold tuxedos. Her gaze rode up the silver escalator with its mahogany handrails, and Molly ruminated on the strange story Mum had told her — about her dad breaking up a fight in the under-fives' toy department...

"Molly?"

A familiar voice made Molly jolt. She turned to see her form tutor, who'd apparently been shopping, accompanied by a group of friends.

"Mrs de Ville." Molly coughed. "Um, how are you?"

"Concerned," said the round-cheeked, dainty-footed teacher. Her friends, talking loudly, hadn't noticed that Doris de Ville had stopped. "Why are you staring at this expensive department store with the shifty face of a shoplifter?"

Mrs de Ville was famously blunt.

"I was just… I was thinking about my dad," Molly blurted. "Apparently he stopped a fight from breaking out here."

Mrs de Ville frowned.

"I'm not lying, Mrs de Ville!" said Molly. "It was in the papers, and…"

"I never said you were lying," Doris said. "I was there."

"Really?" Molly coughed again.

"Yes. Everyone was arguing and shoving, and your father walked over and…"

By now Doris's friends had noticed she wasn't among them. They stopped and shouted for her to hurry up.

"And what, Mrs de Ville?" said Molly.

Doris shrugged. "Nothing — he just … *listened*," she said. "And once everyone had been heard, they didn't seem to want to fight anymore." She waved and moved to join her friends. "See you at school, Molly."

Molly didn't know whether to be satisfied or not with this account. Dad was a chatterbox; she'd imagined him calming everyone with silly jokes and quick wit. With his mouth, not his ears. She was glad to have found out the truth; but suddenly her dad felt more of a mystery to her than ever, and Molly had enough mysteries on her plate.

Rescues

IN THE LOUNGE OF THE EXCELSIOR GUESTHOUSE, a pianist was playing cool jazz. A singer in a suit and shades was crooning into an old-fashioned microphone.

The place was packed.

Howlfair's wealthiest citizens were chattering fabulously in the lounge, in the lobby, up the stairs, in the corridors, in the doorways. Burbling laughter bounced off the walls. The exotic tangled tang of perfumes made the air smell like the arrival of spring on an alien planet. Clinking champagne flutes sang crystal notes. Molly, weaving her way through the crowd in search of Lucinda, encountered her gran slurping pink energy drink from a pint glass.

"Gran, what the heck's going on?"

"It's those journalists," Gran whispered. "They summoned up a toffs' cocktail party *just like that*." She snapped her fingers. "These posh folks are all moving in. They'll be staying at the guesthouse for the next week. And some photographers are here to take glitzy snaps of the Excelsior for *Chunky Chunders* magazine."

"*Country Wonders*," said Molly. "How did the Corches organize the party so quickly?"

"Same way they organized an overnight renovation that turned the place into a five-star hotel," said Gran, taking a slug of pink drink. "Witchcraft."

This struck Molly as a reasonable conclusion. "Where are they?"

"Wafting around," Gran pointed. "Your mother too. She wanted me to talk to them but I'd rather not."

"Don't you trust them?"

"No further than I could throw them."

"Which is probably quite far, if you've been guzzling that energy drink."

Pressing through the throng, Molly passed Mr Banderfrith telling Orson Corches about his antique sword-stick. Orson's expression was unreadable. Molly hurried past, and spotted her mother in the adjoining dining room separated from the lounge by a double archway: she saw the reddish gold of Mum's long, tangled hair bobbing above a sea of glamorous older women with very thin necks. Mum sensed Molly's gaze and turned and waved her over.

"Molly, it's like some mad dream," Mum whispered to her. "That Orson's a bit of a grump — but Lucinda's been singing your praises."

"Really?" said Molly, thinking: *Lucinda won't be singing my praises when I tell her I didn't find the grave she's looking for.*

"She says you've been amazingly ... what's the word she used? *Dedicated*." Mum reached out and uncurled one of Molly's curls, then released it so it coiled again. "You're my hero, Molly Thompson!"

Molly felt herself blushing. Then, as though summoned by the rising heat in Molly's cheeks, Lucinda Corches appeared at her side, wearing a yellow dress with an off-white ruff collar. She looked like a witch-hunter and a witch.

"May I borrow your daughter, Mrs Thompson?"

In the quietest corner of the room, in the shadow of a spike-leaved potted plant, Lucinda addressed Molly with urgency.

"Anything?" she hissed, taking hold of Molly's arm. "Broome? His tomb? Any clues? Any news?"

Molly cleared her throat. "Well, I definitely have some ideas..." She felt the grip tighten. "But I, um, I need to double check some things, so..."

"Double check?" Lucinda's aubergine eyes darkened.

"Molly, we don't have time for double checking. I need to know where to start looking. Orson and I are planning to venture out tonight."

"Tonight?" Molly coughed once more. "The thing is, it seemed like a lot of the books in the library were missing, or there were pages torn out, and..."

The grip tightened. Molly winced.

"What I'm hearing," Lucinda hissed, "is that you've wasted a whole day and we're no closer to finding the Silentman. When Orson hears of this, he'll — *who's this?*"

Suddenly Lucinda removed her claw from Molly's arm.

Turning, Molly saw that Lowry had nudged through the crowd and was approaching with Gabriel in her arms.

"My best friend," said Molly, with some relief.

Her bobbed hair damp from early evening drizzle, Lowry winked at Molly as she strode up to Lucinda. Gabriel glowered.

"Well, hello! I'm Lowry!" She put out her free hand. "Hey, you must be Lucinda Corches, the famous journalist!"

Lucinda, recoiling from Gabriel, was about to speak, but Lowry cut her short.

"I don't know what you've done to the Excelsior,

Lucinda, but it is the absolute vicar's knickers! It's hard to believe that just yesterday this place was a proper run-down dump with a bunch of old people clattering around!"

Again Lucinda opened her mouth to speak, but Lowry babbled on.

"Must've been a mission, cleaning this place up. Molly, why don't you tell me all about it while we go to mine to do homework? Nice to meet you, Lucinda."

With that, Lowry yanked Molly away from the baffled journalist. Gabriel hopped to the ground and led the way.

"Thought I'd rescue you," said Lowry. Gabriel looked over his shoulder and meowed. "Gabriel showed me where to find you. We didn't like the way that weirdly dressed human skyscraper with the teeth was grabbing you. She looks like a Grand National winner wrapped in some curtains."

Lowry led Molly past the buffet table, expertly plucking pastries and dropping them into her schoolbag. She grabbed Molly's ratty rucksack from the coat stand as she pulled her friend through reception and out into the early evening blueness. Gabriel watched.

"Where are you taking me?" Molly said. "What are you doing here?"

"We're meeting Felicity," said Lowry. "We can eat these complicated pastries on the way. I've heard some troubling gossip."

"About what?"

"Carl Grobman," said Lowry. "He's been sent back to the orphanage."

Molly Mode

"I HEARD MY DAD ON THE PHONE THIS afternoon," Lowry told Molly as they made their way to Howlfair Orphanage. A sudden moan of wind tilted the trees along Cecily Craven Street. "He was talking to his boss about something that happened at Mr Wetherill's store. The shop's been closed — that's why Carl had to move back to the orphanage."

"Carl hates the orphanage," Molly said. "He got beaten up all the time there."

"Well, the police have been at Wetherill's store and they've locked the place up. Whatever's happened there, the tourist board wants to keep it secret. I asked Dad about it and — can you believe it! — he sent me to my room without any dinner!"

"Just for asking a question?"

"Yes!" said Lowry, kicking a stone. "And also for eavesdropping on him from behind a door with a cup against my ear. So, anyway, even though I was *literally wasting away* from starvation, I couldn't leave you at Lucinda's mercy." She took another vol-au-vent from her bag and popped it into her mouth. "So I sneaked out of the window and came straight over to rescue you so we could rescue Carl. Or at least find out what's going on. Hey, is that thunder?"

"It's my stomach rumbling."

"You should've had some of your buffet food," Lowry said, wiping her mouth with the back of her hand. "Seriously, those were twelve of the finest pastries I've ever eaten. Maybe Carl can share his orphanage gruel with you. Oh! Speaking of sharing…"

Lowry rummaged in her schoolbag and found a book. She handed it to Molly.

"I asked Dad if he had any books about Howlfair graveyards," said Lowry. "Unbelievably, he did. I said it was for a school project."

The book was titled *Ethelhael Burials*. There was a TOURIST BOARD stamp on a label on the back. "Um, thanks," said Molly. "Does it mention John Broome or the Silentman?"

"Dunno," said Lowry, licking a finger. "But you can use it to help you make up some complicated theory about where to start looking for John Broome's stinky corpse. You can hopefully blag your way into buying

187

yourself more time with Lucinda."

Molly flipped through the pages. "Not bad work, Evans."

"You're welcome. And, hey, sorry about getting you banned from the library. I've been thinking a lot about the whole werewolf thing, and I went into Molly Mode…"

"What's Molly Mode?" said Molly, slipping the book into her backpack. "It sounds like a French fashion shop."

"It's when a problem is vexing my brain and I try to solve it by pretending to be you. I thought: how would Molly research the Kroglin Werewolf if she actually took me seriously? 'Cause obviously I've gone through my family's photo albums, but I've never traipsed round the library looking in, you know, those things that you like…"

"Books."

"That's it — books," said Lowry. "And, well, I don't want to speak too soon, but before you showed up, I managed to do some research and it's looking like you were right — I've been mistaken all along! There isn't a connection between my family and the Kroglins!"

"I've been telling you that for *ages*," said Molly.

"But you never took me seriously enough to bother finding real proof!" said Lowry.

It was true — Molly had always dismissed Lowry's werewolf fears as either silliness or attention-seeking.

"I'm sorry," she said at last.

"What's that?" said Lowry, moving some of her golden bob aside to uncover an ear. "Didn't quite catch that with my non-wolf hearing."

"I said I'm sorry! I promise I'll take you seriously next time you have some mad notion."

Lowry looked very happy.

"So, what changed your mind?" Molly asked. "About the werewolf business?"

They walked past a small park fringed with yew trees. The moon was amber and their footsteps echoed in the cool evening quiet.

"Well, remember how ages ago I found a scribbled family tree in a scrapbook, and it linked my gran to someone called Alicia Hickmott?"

"Course."

"And I found out that Alicia Hickmott was a secret child of one of the Kroglins who got executed for being a werewolf?"

"I remember."

"Well, today I found out that there's another Hickmott in our town! Ailsa Hickmott. No relation to Alicia, as far as I can tell. And I went back and looked at our family tree and ... well, it's scribbly and the ink's run, and now I'm starting to think it might say 'Ailsa', not 'Alicia'. In which case I'm not descended from werewolves! Isn't that brilliant? I feel like I've got my life back and I can stop stockpiling hair removal cream."

"About flipping time."

"I haven't *proven* anything yet, so I can't get too excited. Wouldn't it be awful if my excitement about not being a werewolf turned me into the werewolf that I'm trying to prove I'm not?"

Lowry babbled. Molly listened obligingly; it helped distract her from worrying about seeing Carl again.

The day had dimmed by the time they reached Empty Nest Lane, the steep road on which Howlfair Orphanage waited.

Time to Fly

MOLLY HAD HOPED THAT SINCE THE council had taken over the running of the orphanage following Furlock's disappearance, they would have spruced the place up a bit. But the horrid house remained horrid, a white-walled, black-roofed building with windows painted on, each one framing an illustrated indoor scene of orphans playing. The paint had run, leaving the orphans horror faced, their gaping mouths stretched into screams, their eyes melted into streaks.

"I wish they'd do something about this place," she said. "I can't stand to think of..." She trailed off.

Lowry said, "You can't stand to think of Carl stuck in here, can you?"

Molly ignored her.

"So," said Lowry, clapping. "Shall we wait for Felicity and get her to break in?"

"Let's go round the side. Last time Carl lived here, he gave me a secret signal to call him. The sound of an owl."

"Ooh, how romantic!" grinned Lowry. "And, also, weird."

There may not have been any windows, but there was a door high up on the side of the orphanage — the building had originally been a farmhouse, and the door had been used for putting hay in the loft. The surrounding gardens were overgrown and dominated by hulking oaks.

"Could you help me with the owl noises?" said Molly. "I'm not very good at birdcalls."

It turned out that Lowry wasn't very good at them either. For ten minutes they crouched in the grass making noises.

"Lowry, you're being deliberately rubbish. At least I'm trying."

"Trying what, exactly? You sound like a camel using mouthwash."

Suddenly the high loft door hinged open. A mingling of snickers and shrieks leaked out into the evening. Then a cry:

"You lose again, Grobman! Bye, bye, time to fly!"

The loft was dark, but Molly could just about see a group of children crowding in the high doorway, holding a boy. They'd pushed him to the very edge of the loft and were easing him forward, off balance, then pulling him back just before he lost his footing. It was Carl.

"He's going to fall," Molly gasped — and as she rose and loped through the long grass, she heard a shout from the front of the orphanage:

"Hey!"

She turned to see Felicity Quick running towards her, round the side of the building. There was commotion up in the hayloft. And then, as Molly and Lowry and Felicity collided by the muddy hedge beneath the loft door, a boy fell through the drizzle.

The Vampire Act

CARL GROBMAN'S FALL WAS CUSHIONED BY the shrubs and the bank of mud along the side of the orphanage, and by the three girls he'd fallen onto. The four children thrashed muddily, gasping and cursing. Above them, the cries and gasps of panic turned to laughter and jibes. At last the hayloft door swung shut.

"Why did you shout like that?" Carl rasped at Felicity as he disentangled himself from Molly's backpack. "They wouldn't have dropped me if you hadn't startled them."

Felicity wiped mud off her face with one of the tissues Lowry was handing out. "A better question, Carl, is: why did you just fall out of a window?"

The boy got to his feet, wiping at the mud on his tattered old parka with its fur-lined hood.

"I've got bad news," he said. "Follow me. There's

194

a place I go to in the woods whenever I want a bit of privacy."

"What was going on with those kids?" Lowry asked as they pressed through the darkening woods that led up to the eastern hills. "Do they often fling you from the loft?"

"It's just a game."

"A game where you get thrown out of a loft?"

"Well, that bit's not the game. The game is where they challenge me to stand still while they put spiders on my face, or put my hand over a candle…"

Carl rubbed his hand unconsciously. Molly noticed. "It was the candle game tonight, wasn't it?"

He nodded miserably.

"If I move or make a noise, I have to pay a forfeit. This time the forfeit was being dangled out the hayloft door. They didn't mean to drop me."

Molly followed, her blood boiling.

"You OK, Thompson?" said Felicity. "You've got a face like thunder."

"Just angry," Molly mumbled. "I don't like bullies."

Lowry smirked. She told Carl: "She feels protective about you."

Molly snorted. "Yeah, I always feel protective about people who've tried to kill me."

195

They broke through a wall of Judas-root trees, a creepy-looking species native to Howlfair, and emerged in a thicket carpeted with haunting grey flowers. On the far side was an unusual habitation, a patchwork of plaited twigs and bits of plywood and some fencing and corrugated iron, with a rug for a door. Rain was hitting the canopy of the trees overhead and dripping from the leaves in thick gobs. Carl moved aside the hanging rug door and let the girls into his den.

He switched on a battery-powered plastic lantern that dangled from the roof, illuminating an igloo-shaped room whose walls were hung with fabrics. Across the floor were rugs and cushions and books and a little table, as well as a small rocking chair with a teddy bear sitting on it.

Carl gestured for his guests to sit down. Molly picked a big frayed cushion with tassels.

"How did you find this place?" Lowry asked.

"I made it. A couple of years ago, after Mr Furlock's charity started running the orphanage. Mr Furlock always told us that getting beaten up was character-building — so I'd come here at night to get away from the kids who wanted to …"

"… build your character," said Felicity.

"Yeah."

"But why are you back in the orphanage, Carl?"

196

said Molly. "What happened at Wetherill's shop?"

"The police got an anonymous tip-off," said Carl, sitting down on the chair with the stuffed bear. "Someone told them that Mr Wetherill was keeping real weapons hidden in his shop, so they raided the place and found a load of old muskets. They've taken them away to test if they're dangerous or just antiques. In the meantime, I'm stuck here."

"So who tipped off the police?" Lowry said.

"Could it've been Furlock?" asked Molly.

"He has a motive for getting Mr Wetherill into trouble," said Lowry. "Wetherill helped lose him the elections."

"Things have got proper weird," said Lowry. "Mr Wetherill's been framed, Molly's looking for a dead town crier…"

Carl said, "Dead town crier?"

"Tell him, Thompson," said Lowry.

Molly squirmed. She gave a brief telling of the Silentman legend, and recounted how Lucinda and Orson had persuaded her to help them with a private project — in return for writing a glowing feature about Howlfair and rescuing the Excelsior Guesthouse from ruin.

"So basically," Lowry said to Carl, "she has to help two dodgy journalists find a secret grave."

"There aren't any secret graves in Howlfair," said Carl, frowning. "Haven't you heard of the 1577 Vampire Act?"

The girls looked at him blankly. "The what?" said Molly.

"I suppose it's not really something you'd know about unless you're in the graveyard business." He fiddled with the drawstring of his manky parka. "From 1577, every grave had to be registered, along with their exact locations, so that cases of vampirism could be investigated. Even unmarked graves had to be registered. It was like a census of dead people. The records used to be in the town hall, but now they're hidden somewhere in the crypts under St Fell's Church. I sneaked down once and saw the boxes when I was on flower-arranging duty."

Felicity laughed.

"It's a tourist board thing," Carl snapped. He turned back to Molly. "I've heard that lots of graves were registered under false names, though. So even if you could get the records, they might not help. Anyway, there might not even be anything marking John Broome's grave, just a door in the ground somewhere leading to a hidden tomb. And if it's a secret tomb it'll have all sorts of locks. I doubt even Felicity could break in."

"It'd take more than some ancient old rusty lock to keep me out," Felicity said, affronted. "Not that I'd want to break into someone's tomb, thanks very much."

"I could help," said Carl. He blushed. "I mean, if you wanted my help, I could help. Although I've gotta say, these journalists sound proper suspicious. Are you sure you can trust them?"

"Believe me, Carl, I'm a lot more suspicious than I used to be," Molly said, angry. "I'm very careful who I trust nowadays. Thanks to you."

Carl sighed miserably. *"Fine.* I've accepted that you're never going to forgive me. But just because I was a horrible person in the past, it doesn't mean that I can't help you to —"

"Yes, it does, Carl!" snapped Molly. "It means *exactly that.* You don't get to help me solve mysteries after nearly sacrificing me and my cat to a demon!"

"Time out, time out!" cried Felicity. "Honestly, it's so hard working with you weirdos! Why are we even talking about some ghost story when Wetherill's being hunted by the police? What if Furlock's back in town, and he's got control of his ghouls again?"

"We need to find Mr Wetherill," said Molly. "Does anyone have any idea where he might be?"

"I'm sure he'll get in touch when he thinks it's safe to do so," mumbled Carl.

Molly rose, adjusting her rucksack and brushing the twigs off her jeans, and headed for the makeshift door. "I've got to sneak back into the guesthouse and change out of these muddy clothes and face Lucinda's wrath. I'll see you later."

Carl stumbled after her, following her out into the woods. "Molly?"

She turned. A prong of moonlight, piercing through the trees, caught Carl's eye and made him squint.

"Please don't tell anyone about my hideout. No matter how much you want to get back at me, please keep this place a secret."

Molly tutted. "I'm not a traitor, Carl."

The word *traitor* seemed to stab at Carl's heart; he jolted visibly, and the stricken look on his face made Molly immediately regret saying it. Molly turned to leave before he could see her own face fall; but not before she caught a glimpse of Carl's expression suddenly changing, his features hardening. His dark restless eyes settled. They indicated an unreadable alteration.

Carl had made up his mind about something.

"See you 'round," Molly mumbled, heading off into the night.

Loyalties

THANKS TO GABRIEL, MOLLY MANAGED TO get to her bedroom without anyone noticing that she was covered in dried mud. Having met her outside the Excelsior, Gabriel caused various distractions in the lobby and on the staircase — tripping guests, knocking drinks off tables, appearing unexpectedly in handbags — enabling Molly to slip by without drawing attention. Up in her room, she changed clothes and took out *Ethelhael Burials* and sat at her desk. She worked her way through Lowry's book until she found a section detailing the burial arrangements made for criminals.

"Of course!" Molly said to Gabriel, who was sitting by her lamp, watching her. "John Broome was executed as a criminal, so he won't have been buried in hallowed ground. That rules out the official graveyards. Maybe the mayor buried him in a vault under the town hall? What do you think?"

Gabriel lay down.

"You're right," Molly nodded. "The mayor was lazy. He would've got someone else to bury John Broome. Someone he could trust." She tapped her teeth with a pencil. "I still don't understand why someone like John Broome, who spent his life being nice to people, would turn into an evil phantom when he died. It doesn't make sense."

Gabriel looked up. Moments later there was a knock on the door.

"Molly!" came a voice. "Are you there?" It was Lucinda.

"Here we go," Molly muttered as she threw the book into her desk drawer, and hid Gabriel under her bed. "Come in!"

The door opened wide and a shadow fell across the floor. "Hi, Lucinda," Molly said. "Um, listen — I've been thinking that maybe John Broome is buried in…"

"Howlfair Old Cemetery," Lucinda interrupted.

Molly stared. "Sorry?"

Lucinda followed her shadow into the room. Molly, oppressed by the weight of Lucinda's presence, sat down on her bed.

"When Orson heard you'd made no headway with your investigations, he grew rather enraged." Lucinda sighed splendidly. "He drank three bottles of potion and was violently sick before he had time to make it to the gents' toilets. He had to use the ladies instead."

"Oh, crumbs," said Molly.

"Needless to say, the ladies were not best pleased," said Lucinda. "Some very expensive gowns were ruined this evening. But some good came of it. For the first time in years, Orson heard a voice."

Molly blinked. "From … the dead?"

"Or from his subconscious, or from the deeper fabric of reality — the important thing is that he received *direction*. A voice called him to Howlfair Old Cemetery, and so we are going there tomorrow. At dawn."

"Dawn?" Molly coughed.

"Dawn," said Lucinda curtly. "Have you a vampiric aversion to dawn?"

"Thing is, Lucinda, um, I have cleaning duties."

Lucinda's nostrils flared so widely that Molly felt as though four eyes were glaring down at her. "I will tell your mother to excuse you from your cleaning duties."

Molly squirmed. "It's not Mum who makes me do cleaning. It's, um, a guest."

Lucinda advanced further into the room. "Which guest?"

"Um, does it matter?"

Lucinda's upper lip rolled back to reveal teeth. She bent over and moved her face close to Molly's. Molly heard Gabriel, under the bed, stir with concern.

"We had a deal," hissed Lucinda. "You promised you would belong to me, body and soul, for the duration of our stay. But now I learn that your loyalties are divided."

"No!" Molly said. "Not *divided*, not at all — it's just a favour that I do for Mr Banderfrith, because, um, I don't really have a choice…"

Suddenly Lucinda straightened up. "That old wheezebag Banderfrith!" She brushed down her off-yellow gown. "Not to worry. Our investigations must take place when nobody is around, so if a dawn expedition does not fit with Mr Banderfrith's schedule, we will go at night instead. Nine o'clock. I will make arrangements with your mother. We will address the other matter tomorrow."

Molly chewed a fingernail. "Other matter?"

"Your enslavement by Mr Banderfrith," Lucinda said with venom before striding into the corridor.

After the door had swung shut, Gabriel crept forth and meowed at Molly.

"Me too," she answered, picking him up. "A very bad feeling. You don't think she's going to hurt Banderfrith, do you?"

Gabriel didn't know. He licked his foot.

"And I'm pretty certain that we won't find John Broome buried in the biggest public graveyard in the Ethelhael Valley."

Gabriel looked up at her sadly.

"Yeah, I was thinking that too," she said quietly. "It's where my dad's buried."

Him or Us

I N THE MORNING GLOOM SHE WOKE.
Someone was thumping on her bedroom door.

"Molly, are you awake?" came the voice of Lucinda
Corches from the corridor. "Molly, answer me!"

Disentangling herself from her *Curse of the Mummy*
duvet, Molly croaked, *"Coming!"*

"Hop to it," Lucinda barked. "Orson awaits us in
the lobby. He wishes to speak to you before your …
cleaning duties."

Gabriel scowled as Molly threw on some clothes.
Within the minute, Molly was out of her room and
bumbling after Lucinda, trying not to trip over the
end of the journalist's charcoal-coloured cape as they
descended the green staircase.

Glancing behind her, she noticed Gabriel following
at a distance.

He looked like he knew that something bad was going to happen.

In the lobby, Orson was reading the guestbook with a sour face. Lucinda strode over and exchanged low words with him. Molly lingered by the bannister, chewing a thumbnail.

Orson came over, looking as though he hadn't had a moment's sleep all night. Or all decade.

"Choose," he said gruffly. "Banderfrith or us."

Molly wobbled. "Pardon?"

Orson took another step. His face was all grizzle and stubble and crags.

"Either we leave or he leaves. Choose."

"But ... I can't make someone leave!" said Molly.

"*Him or us*," Orson snarled, his shadow engulfing her. "Do you want him living here?"

"It's not up to me!"

"So you want that rancid little man under your roof?"

"No!" Molly choked, stepping away from him. "No, I flipping don't want him under this roof. I hate him. He hates me. He's a bully and his wigs are like horrid hairy demons! But... But..."

She looked down, pulsing with guilt. When she looked up, Lucinda had joined them.

"Good girl, Molly," Lucinda said. "We got there in the end, didn't we?"

"Take us to his room," said Orson. "Or my sister and I leave now."

From the shadows near the pamphlet shelves, Gabriel watched. What happened next was swift and brutal.

Happy Resolutions

MOLLY MOUNTED THE STAIRS WITH mounting dread. She itched to ask Orson what he was going to do to Mr Banderfrith, but she daren't.

When they arrived at Banderfrith's room, the curtain across the porthole window was undrawn. Molly caught a glimpse of the man fussing around.

Lucinda nodded to Orson, and then each sibling moved to one side of the door.

"Knock," hissed Lucinda.

Molly lifted her hand, hesitated, shuddered. Inside the room, Mr Banderfrith was draping a wig over his head. He stepped back to admire his reflection in the free-standing mirror.

"*Knock*," Lucinda repeated. "We will do the rest." Molly knocked.

* * *

"Molly!" Banderfrith frowned and looked at his watch. "You're actually on time! Ah, I knew I'd train you eventually! Listen, I've been thinking—"

His words were cut short.

Shadows flooded the doorway. The Corcheses swept into the room like vampires.

Banderfrith gasped and staggered as Lucinda closed in on him, her cape lofting. It was as though he saw something unspeakable in her face.

"Turn around and face the wall," Orson ordered Molly. "Close your eyes. My sister will tell you when you can look again."

Molly felt unable to disobey. She turned to face the wall, standing in front of Mr Banderfrith's collection of walking sticks, one of which — she could see the silver handle — allegedly contained a sword.

She closed her eyes.

She didn't want to see what she had just unleashed on the guesthouse's oldest resident.

But she could still *hear*.

She could hear Lucinda whispering rapidly in a serpentine tone.

She could hear Mr Banderfrith whimpering.

She thought she heard Gabriel, outside the room, meow. Then Molly heard Orson storm from the room and hiss at the cat.

What have I done?

Lucinda placed a hand on her shoulder. "It's over, Molly," she cooed. "Mr Banderfrith will be leaving tonight and taking up residence elsewhere in superb alternative lodgings." She turned Molly around as though they were on a gameshow and Molly was finding out what she'd won. "Is that all right with you, Mr Banderfrith?"

Mr Banderfrith was standing in front of his desk with a macabre smile on his face. He looked like a corpse whose expression has been rearranged by a mad mortician. His eyes looked wet and unseeing. He nodded like a puppet.

"Good!" Lucinda said brightly, pushing Molly towards the door. "I love happy resolutions."

In the corridor, Orson was not to be seen. Molly was shaking.

"Lucinda," she said, "what just happened?"

"You just learned that Orson and I will not share you with anyone else," said Lucinda. "And we will not accept any dilution of the terms of our agreement. Do you understand?"

Molly nodded unhappily.

"Excellent," said Lucinda, striding down the corridor.

Molly followed.

"No need to thank me for freeing you from the old man's tyranny. Orson and I will organize his removal. All you need to do is spend today enjoying your freedom. We have a big night ahead of us."

"But … what did you say to him?"

"I made him an offer," said Lucinda, dismissing further discussion about Banderfrith with a wave of painted nails. "Now, forget about that old windbag. We leave for the cemetery at nine tonight, and we will find out what the great Molly Thompson is made of!"

As soon as Lucinda had sailed off to her room, the woman's warning came to Molly's mind: *we will not accept any dilution of the terms of our agreement.*

What would the Corcheses do to Lowry and Felicity and Carl if they found out that Molly had told them about the Silentman?

Molly ran downstairs. She had an urgent call to make.

Message in the Guestbook

IN THE MORNING COOL OF THE LOBBY, ORSON Corches was speaking gruffly on the white and gold telephone.

"Tonight. Ten o'clock. Removals. Room eighty-two." He paused. "No — the *other* kind of removal."

From behind the coat stand, Gabriel listened. After Orson hung up, the cat slipped away.

Now Molly padded down the stairs — and Orson, hearing, dashed for the coat stand. He crouched behind the hanging fur coats and watched Molly cross the tiles to the telephone.

Molly picked up the phone and dialled.

"Lowry, it's urgent," she said when her best friend answered sleepily.

"It'd better be," Lowry yawned. "Hey, before I forget, can you come over tonight? I've found some books in my dad's study that might help you with your Silentman thing."

"Can't — I'm going to the Old Cemetery at nine with the Corcheses," said Molly. "Actually, the Silentman's what I need to talk to you about. Listen — nobody can know that I've told you about him, or about the Corcheses' project, OK?"

"Fine by me."

"Can you call Felicity and tell her to keep quiet too?"

"Course," said Lowry. "What about Carl?"

Molly chewed her lip. "I'm guessing Carl doesn't speak to anyone anyway. But, um, if you see him, tell him to keep quiet too…"

"Molly, is everything OK with you and the Corcheses?" Lowry asked. "Did you manage to win them over? Or … are you in some sort of trouble?"

Molly thought about the graveyard. About the potion. "Everything's fine," she said, unaware that Orson Corches was listening, scowl faced, nearby. Then she added, "Ask me again tomorrow."

As Molly replaced the handset, she noticed a pencil with an eraser sitting by the guestbook and knew immediately that Carl had visited. He'd left a message for her in the guestbook once before — just prior to leading her into Benton Furlock's trap — and

214

she would scrub it out after reading.

Frowning, not sure what to expect, she opened the guestbook — and she buckled with when she saw the message Carl had inscribed.

Can't stay in orphanage and
I am not wanted anywhere so
I am going to disappear.
Don't expect to ever see me
again.
Carl

Hurriedly she rubbed out the message. But she couldn't erase the image of his stricken face outside his den after she'd skewered his heart with the word traitor. She couldn't erase from her mind the look of grim resolve that had settled on his features.

She whispered, "What the heck have I done?"

The Girl with the
Tomb-Seeking Hair

OVER A DINNER OF VERY FANCY DISHES
served by the silent waiters and waitresses
that the Corcheses had installed in the guesthouse,
Lucinda asked Mum if Molly was free to provide a
tour of Howlfair by moonlight that evening, and Mum
hesitantly agreed. Gabriel, however, proved less keen
on Molly going out. When she tried to get ready after
dinner, he mewled and leapt into her wardrobe and
sat on her jumpers and hissed.

"For Pete's sake, Gabriel, I have to go," she said,
wrestling him out of the wardrobe. "If you're so
bothered about me going out, just follow me and do
your usual trick of lurking nearby to check I'm OK.
OK?"

Gabriel ran in front of the door and glared.

Molly climbed into a jumper. The Howlfair wind

216

breathed on the window and jostled the frame. "You think the Corcheses will try to get me to drink their potion, don't you?"

Gabriel sniffed twice.

"Listen, Gabriel, I don't need some mad potion to find their secret grave when I've got *this*." She tapped her head. "Obviously I'm referring to my brain, not my hair. My hair couldn't find a secret grave. And as for the Corcheses: I know they're not nice people. They might even be *bad* people. But sometimes you have to give bad people a chance."

Gabriel grumbled.

"Don't give me that *So why didn't you give Carl another chance?* look. It's not my fault that he's gone all melodramatic and flounced off."

She was sure she heard Gabriel tut.

"OK, OK, I'll try to find him! I'll do it as soon as this Silentman business is over. But right now I've *got to go*."

She strode to the door and wrenched it open, so that Gabriel had to skittle out of the way. She felt a pulse of guilt.

"Look, I know you're just trying to protect me," she said, kneeling and patting his head. "But there's nothing to worry about." She stood up. "I'm not going to drink that potion — cause I don't need to. If Orson's

217

ghost voices were right about John Broome being in Howlfair Old Cemetery, then I'm going to find that flipping grave. I'm going to show the Corcheses what I'm made of."

Then she slipped from the room, giving her scowling cat a weak smile, and headed downstairs to where Lucinda and Orson were waiting.

The Hands of Liars

DOWNSTAIRS, MUM AND GRAN WERE arguing next to one of the huge copper fire extinguishers that had been installed during the refurbishment.

"What's going on?" said Molly.

"What's going on," said Mum, "is that I caught your grandmother pulling a fire extinguisher off the wall."

"I just wanted to see if I could lift it," Gran grumbled.

The fitting had broken and the extinguisher was leaning against the wall. "No point having fancy fire extinguishers if they're too heavy to wield in battle." She sized up the fire extinguisher as though it were a wrestling opponent. "Molly, help us get this back on the wall, will you?"

"She doesn't have time," Mum said. "Molly, the Corcheses are waiting for you downstairs."

As soon as Molly arrived in the lobby, Orson strode to the white and gold telephone and made a call. Within minutes a rather regal-sounding horn tooted from the forecourt, and while Lucinda roughly straightened Molly's coat collar, Orson opened the front door of the guesthouse to reveal not one but two black and chrome saloon cars with hatted drivers.

"Why do we need two cars?" Molly asked.

"I'm hoping we don't," said Lucinda cryptically. "Let's go."

Soon, once again, Molly was being chauffeured through the streets in the purring car. She glanced briefly over her shoulder and saw the headlights of the second saloon close behind.

"Molly," said Lucinda, fanning her fingers and looking at the phases of the moon on her nails. "Tell me the truth. Have you told anyone about our project?"

Molly felt her throat tighten. Her face burned. Outside the windows, the dark town slid by in a blur of crooked trees and empty staring shops and the ectoplasmic glow of street lamps.

"It's a simple yes or no question," Lucinda said. "Have you kept to the terms of our agreement or not?"

Molly saw the driver looking at her in the rear-view mirror with amusement.

220

She had to lie. After what had happened to Mr Banderfrith, she couldn't risk putting her friends in jeopardy.

"Yes," she said at last. "I haven't told anyone."

Lucinda nodded. "I'm glad," she said. "A person should not put her fortunes in the hands of liars."

The driver smirked. Suddenly Lucinda looked out of the window and clapped excitedly.

"Ah — *nous sommes arrivés!*"

They had indeed arrived, but not at the cemetery.

Broken Corcheses

THE CAR TURNED ONTO THE DRIVEWAY OF one of the few guesthouses in Howlfair not located on Cecily Craven Street. It was a mournful building of faded pink and brown stone with a tall roof of scalloped slates. The place had always suggested to Molly a haunted gingerbread house. It was officially famous for having (supposedly) once accommodated a demon who could (allegedly) turn into a thundercloud, and who attracted a group of followers who were (predictably) witches, a group who took over the guesthouse for a few weeks in the late seventeenth century and caused havoc conjuring the demon, which would fly out of the chimney and attack locals on their way to St Fell's Church. Unofficially the place was famous for having lots of rats.

"But — this is the Blowbridge Tavern."

"Yes, Molly. Orson and I will be moving in here.

We will arrange for our things to be delivered tomorrow. Our other driver will take you back to the Excelsior, which we will of course return to its former state…"

Again the driver was smirking. He brought the car to a halt on the gravel; the other car followed suit.

Molly's chest was a-buzz with swarming panic. "Sorry, Lucinda, but I don't understand. Why —"

"'Cause you lied," growled Orson.

"And because you betrayed us," added Lucinda coolly.

"I — what?"

"You told your friends about our mission, and then you lied about it on the way here."

Molly didn't know what to say. She had no idea how the Corcheses had found her out, and there seemed little point in trying to extend the deception. So what could she say?

"I — I had to!" she ventured as the driver got out and opened the door for Lucinda.

"Of *course* you did," yawned Lucinda, swinging a leg from the car.

"No, I mean, I thought they could … help!" Molly improvized as Lucinda angled herself from the vehicle and stretched luxuriously, briefly framing the moon between her raised arms. "Felicity's an amazing

223

locksmith, so I thought she could help us break into the tomb, and Lowry, um, has a dad who…"

She heard the sound of sliding pages, and turned to see Orson leafing through a notepad. "A dad who works for the tourist board," he said. "Then there's Carl Grobman, who …"

"… who knows all about graveyards and tombs because he works as a gravedigger!" cried Molly. "I mean, he's a sort of *pretend* gravedigger — it's an act he does for tourists — but…"

But now Lucinda was heading for the other black saloon, whose driver was unloading fancy black leather suitcases on wheels. As Molly tumbled from the car, Lucinda snatched a heavy suitcase with each hand and began to lug them towards the house, Molly loping after her and gushing excuses, and then —

And then Lucinda suddenly released the suitcases and crumbled to the ground, her knees crunching into the gravel of the forecourt.

Molly halted. She looked around at the drivers of the cars, who were standing frowning, confused. Orson watched with bored eyes through a car window. Molly called, "Lucinda?"

She thought she heard quiet sobs.

Tentatively she approached.

"Lucinda?"

After some more whispery weeping, Lucinda gave a loud sniff.

She took a breath and said: "Molly Thompson, you have broken me."

Molly said, "Huh?"

Lucinda Corches shook her head solemnly and ranked her claws through the gravel. "We should never have come here," she hissed. "I should never have given you this opportunity. I trusted you, and at every turn you have defied me. And now... And now..."

She wrestled with a sob and buckled inside the frame of her gown. A cello wind woke the treetops around the forecourt and made them sizzle.

"Lucinda?" said Molly, treading carefully around the demolished woman and pausing before her. "Are you OK?"

New strains of wind joined the cello. Violas, flutes.

"I will tell you my deepest fear," said Lucinda, wiping her aubergine-coloured eyes. "Yes. I will tell you what I have not told anyone else in the world, and then you will see how you have cut me to the heart." She lifted her olive face. "I will tell you the whole truth behind our search for the Silentman."

Worth Killing For

WHILE THE DRIVERS KEPT A RESPECTFUL distance and Orson tried to catch up on his beauty sleep in the back of his saloon, Lucinda spoke softly to Molly, almost tenderly, beneath the moony night.

"I told you that our parents died before they could trace the origins of the Silentman myth," she said. "The truth is that we do not know what happened to them. Orson and I never knew where they went on their travels. They never told us of their findings. One night, when I was eleven and Orson was twelve, Orson ventured downstairs for a glass of milk and he overheard our parents talking about how they'd found the town where the legend originated and were going to see a tomb that contained wonders. The next day, they left my brother and me with our governess, and travelled there."

"To Howlfair."

"Yes. After many years of tracking the Silentman's tale here, to its source, Orson and I have discovered that my parents came to Howlfair. And they never returned. They were never seen again."

Molly noticed that one or two faces were peering out from lit windows on the face of the Blowbridge Tavern. If Lucinda had noticed them too, she seemed not to care.

"They left notebooks, boxes of receipts, maps," Lucinda went on. "I sifted through them endlessly, trying to find out where my parents were travelling to before they disappeared." Suddenly Lucinda riveted Molly with a glare. "Molly, my fear is that someone didn't want my parents to find that tomb — or someone wanted to punish them for seeking it. My fear is that they were … *murdered*."

Molly gasped. "Here in Howlfair?"

"Here in Howlfair," said Lucinda. "That's why I want to know what's in that tomb. I want to know if it is something worth killing for. I want to solve the mystery of my parents' disappearance. And *that* is why I was so desperate to keep our mission secret. If someone is guarding that tomb — if someone killed my parents — I don't want to end up dead too."

Molly looked away. "I'm sorry…"

Lucinda sighed. Nodded. Then she reached inside her handbag as the wind filled the surrounding trees with booming whooshes. She took out a bottle of purple potion.

"The potion is not for the faint of heart," Lucinda said. "It opens one up to strange realities. To *truth*." She held up the bottle so that Molly could see the moonlit liquid swirl. "But it wears off quickly, and there are no after-effects. What you have to decide — right now, if you want me to forgive your betrayal — is whether my truth is worth your trouble."

"You mean, um…"

"My brother and I can move into this … *cosy-looking* tavern and continue our quest without you — and you can be assured that our feature for *Country Wonders* will not speak highly of the Excelsior Guesthouse — or you can earn yourself one last chance to help my brother and me complete our mission. By drinking the potion in this bottle."

Molly chewed her lip. "Um, about this potion…"

"Decide," said Lucinda, slowly rising to full height and holding out the bottle. "Right now."

Molly knew she had no choice. She'd bungled things royally by telling Felicity and Lowry and Carl about the Corcheses' search for the Silentman. Yet again she'd put her mum's guesthouse in jeopardy. It was up to her to put things right, even if that meant drinking some weird potion. It was a gamble — but it was no more a gamble than the gamble she'd asked Lowry to take earlier that year, when she'd persuaded her to drink an anti-werewolf potion. Why would she expect her friends to do things she wasn't willing to do herself?

"I'll do it," Molly mumbled.

Lucinda smiled. "I knew you would see sense eventually."

Molly tried to blink her dread away. She took a breath and reached for the potion.

Before her fingers could close around the bottle of purple liquid, Lucinda snatched it away.

"Not yet," said Lucinda. "Get in the car, Molly. I have a surprise for you."

Quicksilver

IN A MESSY OVERTURNED BEDROOM — ROOM eighty-two of the Excelsior Guesthouse — Gabriel stood on a desk, meowing as loud as he could. Trying to wake Mr Banderfrith.

Gabriel nudged Mr Banderfrith's face with his head. He dug his claws into Banderfrith's scalp. It was hopeless. No matter what Gabriel did, Banderfrith barely stirred. The eyes fluttered; the hands grasped weakly; the mouth uttered a moan; but that was all.

Gabriel looked at the old man's watch. He remembered what Orson had said on the telephone.

Tonight. Ten o'clock. Removals. Room eighty-two.

And the words that had chilled Gabriel:

No — the OTHER kind of removal.

Molly nestled between the smug silent journalists as the car conveyed them to Howlfair Old Cemetery, her eyes on the purple bottle that Lucinda was toying with in the manner of a stage magician (palming it, making it disappear and reappear). The streets moved by. Molly wondered why they were taking such an odd route to the cemetery — the higgledy-piggledy Number 6 bus route, actually. She wondered what Lucinda's surprise would be. And then the car pulled over beside the bus stop outside Clutchley's Delicatessen; and a new wondering arose, one so strong that Molly could not help but blurt it out. "What the heck are Lowry and Felicity doing at the bus stop?"

The driver, leaving the engine running, exited the car and opened the rear door for Lucinda to get out. Lucinda waved Molly out of the car.

"Ask them yourself."

"What's going on?" Molly asked, while Lucinda waited by the car and scrutinized her talons.

"Lucinda phoned us earlier," said Lowry, leaning against the wooden bus shelter. "She asked us to sneak out and meet you here — she knows that you told us about her secret mission."

"She said she's got an idea where John Broome is buried," said Felicity. "She wants us to help you find the exact spot and break into his tomb while she and her brother hide nearby. That way, if someone catches

231

us trying to break in, it'll just look like some meddling kids helping meddling Molly Thompson with her latest bit of meddling."

"She said if we didn't agree, she and her brother were going to move out of your guesthouse and write a horrid article about it," said Lowry.

"And you both — you both said yes?" asked Molly. "You agreed to help me *break into a tomb*?"

"Yeah, I must be going soft," said Felicity. "I've decided lately that I'm going to try to be a better and more helpful person — and what better way to improve oneself than to steal a bag of tools and break into someone's final resting place?"

"As for me," said Lowry, "as soon as Lucinda asked if I wanted to spend my evening unearthing a tomb, I immediately agreed to check my diary. And what do you know, it turned out that my previous graverobbing appointment had been cancelled!"

Molly shook her head. "Thank you, Lowry. Thank you, Felicity. You guys are —"

"Stupid?" said Felicity. "Suicidal? Just promise me that a terrifying phantom isn't going to grab us and drive us mad."

"The phantom is trapped in a snuffbox at the bottom of the Six Bridges Stream. We'll just be looking for John Broome's remains. And an antique handbell that may or may not be magical."

"Well, as fun as this sounds, I should warn you that I can't stay out all night," said Lowry. "If my parents catch me crawling back in at six a.m., I too will end up in a snuffbox at the bottom of the Six Bridges Stream."

"We'll be quicker than quicksilver," said Molly.

Lucinda called over, "Time to go, girls!"

"Thanks for doing this, you two," said Molly as she and her friends headed to their cars. "If we're lucky, this whole business will be over by midnight."

But of course Molly was not counting on luck. She would have to drink the Corcheses' sinister potion.

"Molly, you're riding with me," Lucinda called. "Lowry and Felicity, you're in the car behind."

Fatal Folly

"So ... WHAT EXACTLY HAPPENS WHEN I drink this?" Molly asked Lucinda, trying to stop her hand from shaking.

As the purring car with the hatted driver conveyed her to the graveyard where her own father was buried, her friends following in the second car, Molly absent-mindedly traced the scratches on her arms from where Gabriel had tried to prevent her from leaving the guesthouse. In one hand she held the apothecary bottle filled with the swirling purple potion. The navy evening streaked by.

"Ah, it's been many years since my first draught," Lucinda sighed. "How to describe the sensation? *A veil drops.* A veil you never knew existed. Between this world and the world of the unseen."

"Dead people speak to you," said Orson. "They babble nonsense at you till you ask them a question.

234

So ask them questions. Preferably: *where in this godforsaken boneyard is John Broome?*"

"How soon before it wears off?" Molly asked.

"A matter of minutes," said Lucinda. "So be quick to ask your questions."

"And the dead ... do they try to trick you?"

"I don't believe you are contacting the dead directly," said Lucinda. "I believe you are connecting with the traces of knowledge they left behind, imprinted on the fabric of the unseen. This connection takes the form of a conversation, because that is what our minds are most comfortable with."

Orson blew a raspberry. "Nah, you definitely talk to the dead."

"We agree to disagree on the subject," said Lucinda. "It's best, Molly, if you experience the potion for yourself."

Weirdly, the longer Molly looked at the bottle in her hand, the less threatening the swirling potion seemed. She was surprised to find that she felt a twinge of desire for its contents. A thirst.

Lucinda said, "Uncork the bottle."

Suddenly it didn't seem barmy of Molly to be pulling the cork stopper from a bottle of creepy potion that would make her hear ghosts.

Lucinda said, "Drink."

It did not seem reckless for Molly to be bringing the rounded lip of the bottle to her mouth.

"That's it, Molly. Nearly there."

It did not seem dangerous to be tilting her head back while Lucinda looked on.

She drank; and it did not seem fatal folly to let the potion in.

The Purple Potion

AFTER SHE'D SWALLOWED THE LAST DROP, the car lifted gently and began to fly. That's how it felt to Molly, anyway. As though she were aboard a flying coach pulled by phantom horses.

Hooded clouds escorted the vehicle. Lucinda and Orson and the driver became featureless shadows. The air inside the car grew grainy. Ghost faces emerged from the static, looked at Molly with shameless curiosity, then faded.

"Sign this," said Orson gruffly, passing her a pen and what looked like a contract written on yellow vellum. Her vision swam. She thought she saw the words "hereby" and "absolve" and "fire" and "fury" and "Lowry Evans" and "Felicity Quick" and "untimely death". Without knowing what she was doing, she set the pen nib to the paper, which was balanced on one knee. She caught herself.

237

"Wait, what is this?" she said. It was hard to speak. She felt like she was talking in her sleep.

"Just some legal business," said Lucinda sweetly.

Molly felt a sudden sickly aversion to signing the document, and she tried to snatch away her hand, but gasped as a wispy ethereal skeletal claw seemed to manifest beside her own; it wrapped itself around her hand and seemed to spirit her into unwilled motion; she felt herself inscribe a venal version of her own signature, and when she was done Lucinda thanked her and whipped the contract away.

I shouldn't have signed that bit of paper, Molly thought. *I shouldn't have drunk that potion.*

I shouldn't have come out tonight.

The car continued to fly, and finally landed (or stopped) outside Howlfair Old Cemetery. The moon was the same colour as the hillside mist. Everything glowed. The second car stopped beside the gates and released Lowry and Felicity, whose winter jacket was concealing her father's locksmith's bag.

"Are you OK?" Lowry shouted as Molly toppled from the car.

"She's fine," Lucinda called as she helped Molly find her feet.

A skeletal face poked through the fabric of Molly's mind and she buckled, whimpering. She closed her eyes. She heard voices immediately. She realized that they belonged to Felicity and Orson arguing at the gate. Molly tried to screen them out. She heard Lucinda walk away. Then, suddenly, her skull began to fill with whispers, barely comprehensible.

"Please," she thought, *"show me where to find the tomb of John Broome."*

More whispers.

Bored, angry, desperate, lonely, mischievous whispers.

She wondered if she should have asked the dead to tell her where Broome was buried, rather than to show her.

She opened her eyes.

Lucinda was opening the cemetery gate while Orson fiddled with a camera.

Lucinda beckoned Molly over.

"Are you ready to join us?" she called.

Then, as the gate swung open in a small storm of sickly fog, Molly's heart hiccupped. Across the hillside beyond, the grave mist had risen to form human shapes, with mouths gaping and fingers long. And these wraiths, like Lucinda, were beckoning.

Where the Dead Led

SILENTLY THE DEAD LED MOLLY THROUGH the graveyard; and Molly led her companions.

"Molly, where are we going?" Lowry whispered, moving alongside her. "Also, why do you seem like you know the way?"

"*Also*," said Felicity, "why are you suddenly acting weirder than a blue goose?"

Lowry cleared her throat. "Is it because, you know, your dad is buried here?"

Molly forced herself to shake her head. The ghosts of green mist reared up and raised crooked claws and pointed the way. Whenever Lowry or Felicity or Lucinda or Orson inadvertently walked into one — it seemed that only Molly could see them — they dissipated, then reformed. Overhead, the evening sky dressed itself for night.

"We're close," Molly managed to mumble.

* * *

"Are you sure this is it?" said Lucinda as Molly led the group towards a fenced-off tomb on the edge of a thicket of fog-swaddled trees. The heavy wooden door seemed too small for an adult to get through. On top of the monument was a statue of a hooded skeleton, no bigger than Molly, turning to beckon someone to follow it somewhere. From the trees came the woody warnings of owls.

"I'm sure," whispered Molly, looking up at what Lowry and Felicity and Lucinda and Orson could not see: the two rows of misty spectres who'd formed an alley leading to the tomb's gate, and who were ushering Molly towards it with ragged hands.

As soon as the group reached the tomb, the phantoms —

— *vanished*.

The whispers were still in Molly's head, but she felt more lucid now, more in control.

She stood up straight. She took a deep breath. She began to move towards the tomb.

"I may grow emotional," said Lucinda. "To be here at last! Orson, we're really here!"

Orson, watching from beside the statue of the skeleton-child, sniffed meaningfully.

"I don't flipping like this one bit," said Lowry.

The gate was unlocked. Felicity and Lucinda and Lowry followed Molly through. Orson joined them as Felicity tried to open the tomb door.

"Locked," he said.

"Thanks for your input," Felicity tutted. "I can see it's locked."

"How easy will it be to break in?" Lucinda said.

"I can do it," said Felicity. "Look at the locks. These silver seals here with the markings. They're meant to keep ghouls out, not grave robbers."

"I prefer the term dead-meddlers," said Lowry.

"Break them," Lucinda said.

Deep Breaths

FELICITY PRISED AT THE SEAL. A CONCEALED lock surrendered and she pulled open the small, squeaking door. An ancient stench arose.

Stone steps descended into a blackness so utter it seemed solid. As though you'd bump your nose if you walked into it. Molly could hear the voices of the dead rising, tangled, from the tomb.

Lucinda handed her a torch. Molly struggled to keep her hands from quaking as she took it. She switched it on, expecting something like the blinding beam of her beloved Shadeshifter Tactical Flashlight to blast out, but a dribble of lazy light was all it conjured. She aimed the beam down the staircase. The steps rounded a corner and vanished towards who knew what.

"I'm not sure I'll fit down there," said Lowry in a tiny voice. The passageway was dreadfully low and narrow. "I may look small, but I expand when I'm, um, underground."

"Shut up, Lowry," said Felicity.

Orson delved into one of his shoulder bags and pulled out an instant camera. "Take this," he said to Molly, hanging it around Molly's neck by its strap. "I want to see photographs of the Silentman's tomb." He gave her a cloth shoulder bag. "Put them in here."

Molly tried to take a step towards the tomb but her frightened legs buckled. She dropped the bag on the grass. She stooped to pick it up and dropped the torch. Then she picked up the torch and dropped both torch and bag.

"Deep breaths, Thompson," tutted Felicity. "I'll hold the torch."

Molly gave her a shaky smile of gratitude and looped the strap over her shoulder and handed Felicity the torch.

"But you're going first," Felicity added.

The Sense of Fear

THE TORCHLIGHT SHAKILY ILLUMINATED the stone steps as Molly, hunched double because of the low tunnel, progressed around the curve in the staircase. She braced herself for that moment when, turning the corner, she would face total darkness until Felicity (who was descending feet-first with the torch, as though sledging) and Lowry, who was whimpering, caught up.

The voices of the dead grew louder — but still not loud enough for Molly to hear the words they were saying.

Then a louder voice made Molly jolt.

It was just Lowry complaining.

"Why did they make these tunnels so flipping snug?"

"To put off casual visitors," Molly said. "Like grave robbers."

"But couldn't grave robbers just send children to do their robbing? Kind of like those journalists up there are doing?"

Molly halted. Some of the whispers in her head were getting loud enough to understand.

She thought she heard the word *free*.

"Yes — but children scare easily," she said. "So wherever there are narrow tunnels in tombs, you usually find that the makers installed devices to deter children…"

"Like what?"

"Like *fear sensors*."

"What!" coughed Lowry. "Why didn't you tell us about the fear sensors?"

"Because I just remembered," said Molly with growing dread.

She ran her hand along the wall. Soon she located a round copper plate with engravings. "Oh, crumbs."

"What? What is it?" babbled Lowry.

"I think I found one."

Flipping Close

"MOLLY THOMPSON, THIS THING ABOUT fear sensors is the kind of thing you either say *before* we go into a tomb or keep to yourself until after we're *out* of the tomb," said Lowry, peering at the disc-shaped copper device set into the wall. "Now I'm *definitely* going to get scared, and then — wait, what happens if you set one off? How do fear sensors work?"

Molly shook her head. "No one knows how they work. They were illegal to sell, but you could get them on the black market. A vicar of St Fell's denounced them as made by demons, and he tried to break one open to see how it worked, but poisonous gas came out and killed him."

"Actually, her other question was the more important one," said Felicity. *"What're they gonna do to us?"*

"They'll be old and rusty. They probably won't

work. But if we do set one off, we'll probably get locked in or something." She looked at Felicity over her shoulder. "Whatever's in that crypt, we can't let ourselves get too scared."

"Are you insane?" Lowry laughed manically. "Why are we still even going ahead with this?"

Molly pointed at the small wooden door at the tunnel's end. "Because we're so flipping close! Through that door is the end of this stupid Silentman business. But we've got to go through it and take some snaps of John Broome's skeleton and whatever treasures are buried there, OK?"

"But what if his ghost — the Silentman's — is in there too?"

"He won't be!" sighed Molly. "I told you, he's in a snuffbox at the bottom of the Six Bridges Stream!"

"Hate to admit it, but I'm feeling a bit spooked by this too," said Felicity. "And so are you, Thompson. Your hair is actually on end."

"It actually is!" exclaimed Lowry. "I thought that only happened in cartoons."

Molly tutted and patted her hair down. "Fine — both of you go back. Give me the torch and I'll do this myself."

Felicity and Lowry exchanged looks. At last Lowry gave a long, pained sigh. "Just lead the way."

Molly arrived at the crypt door, swimming through a net of cobwebs. By dim torchlight she gave the door a push, expecting it to be locked or at least stiff. Instead, with a scandalized squeal, it swung open as though aided by an unseen hand. Immediately the voices in Molly's head grew louder.

Free…

Free…

Her throat raw, Molly crawled into the burial chamber.

Cryptic

THE VAULT WAS OVAL, SPACIOUS, WITH DUST and cobwebs covering the floor up to knee-height.

It seemed empty. Except…

Plaques on the walls. With writing.

Molly took a photo. The crypt exploded with light from the flashbulb.

"Can you warn me before you do that?" hissed Felicity.

Molly removed the instant photo, waggled it, and slipped it into her cloth bag.

"Oh, God, do you think he's buried in the wall?" Lowry asked, following Molly into the vault.

"Let's find out."

Moving around the edge of the room, wading through the dust, sending evil white clouds billowing, Molly gestured for Felicity to point the torch at the first plaque. She took another instant photo; again the white flash and the noise of the photo popping from the front of the camera made Felicity jump.

"Keep calm," said Molly, putting the photograph in the bag. "Remember the fear sensors."

The plaque read:

> SEEKEST THOU GRAVE-LOOT,
> CHILD? HEREIN IS NONE OF WHICH TO
> TELL. BUT IF THOU HAST HITHER BEEN
> SENT IN SEARCH OF JOHN BROOME
> AND HIS BELL — TREAD ON.

"Seems they want any child grave robbers to know there's nothing here worth stealing," said Molly.

"Drat," said Lowry. "I'd hoped to come out of this with a new laptop."

Molly tramped on, raising dust. To the next plaque. She took a photo — Felicity winced at the hot flash — and dropped it into the bag. She read the inscription.

> BURIED NOT DEAD BUT DEAD OF EYE
> HERE ARE HID HIS QUARRIE LEFT
> TO MOULDER — AN EVIL FATE
> YET A NECESSITIE

"His quarrie?" muttered Molly. "Whose quarry? The Silentman's quarry?"

Lowry was trying not to choke on the dust. "He's got a quarry? Like a stone quarry?"

"Quarry also means *prey*."

"Huh?"

"The Silentman's victims were buried here," whispered Molly. "And it sounds like they weren't quite dead."

The voices in her mind grew louder.

... *will set the* ...

... *freeee* ...

... *she will* ...

... *freee* ...

"But where?" hissed Felicity. "Where are they?"

Molly wasn't listening. She edged along the wall to the next plaque. Took a photo.

HE IS HID
AND GUARDED WITH
A RIDDLE

"This is too weird," said Lowry. "Is his dead body here or not? Are his victims here or not? Where's he hid? Where's this riddle?"

"Lowry, please, try to calm down," said Molly. "According to the legends, John Broome was buried with his victims. So as long as the victims are here somewhere, we're in the right place."

She wobbled over to the next plaque, taking another photograph and bagging it diligently.

WHERE LIETH JOHN BROOME?
NOT IN A GRAVEYARD.
BUT RESOLVE MY RIDDLE
AND THOU WILT KNOW:
I FILL AS I EMPTY
I EMPTY AS I FILL
YET NOTHING LEAVETH ME
AND NOTHING ENTERETH.
WHAT AM I?

"Why are riddles and people who invent riddles so ridiculous?" said Lowry. "How can something filleth and emptieth if nothing leaveth it or entereth?"

Molly shook her head. The ghosts in her mind seemed to be reaching out and snatching away her thoughts before she could organize them against the riddle's logic. "I can't figure it out."

Felicity said, "I thought you were, like, the queen of riddles?"

Molly thought: *Yeah, when my head isn't full of the voices of the restless dead.* "Let's worry about the riddle when we've got out of here," she said. "If John Broome isn't buried in a graveyard, then this can't be his tomb. But if his victims are buried here, then the old legend about Broome being buried with his victims is wrong. Whoever built this tomb knew that people would come here searching for Broome's remains, and they left clues about where to find them, but they're buried somewhere else. Come on — there's one more plaque."

The voices of the dead weren't speaking anymore. They were sniggering at the back of her mind.

Molly should have recognized it as a warning.

She started to move towards the final plaque.

"You know what I don't get?" Lowry said, moving along the wall, Felicity's torchlight weaving. "If the tomb of John Broome is supposed to be secret, why did someone put a riddle in this tomb telling people where to find him?"

"Maybe they reckon that nobody who comes down here will ever solve the riddle," said Felicity.

Molly stopped in front of the plaque. The words were covered in a layer of dust. She reached out and started to brush the dust away.

Then she froze with terror.

"Or maybe," she whispered, "they knew that nobody who comes down here will ever leave."

Riddle While You Burn

WITHOUT THINKING, MOLLY DREW HER hand once more across the square metal plaque to uncover the inscription — and she heard a click from behind it.

The message on the last plaque was:

> SEEKER OF THE FORBIDDEN TOMB
> I GAVE THEE CHANCE TO TURN
> NOW TIME ENOUGH IN HELL HAST
> THOU TO RIDDLE AND TO BURN

Now something was whirring within the walls.

"Holy haddocks, what the heck's that?" Lowry cried.

"It's a trap," Molly said shakily. "Guys, something's about to scare us — *and we can't let ourselves get scared. We can't set off the fear sensors.*"

For a second it seemed that the walls were beginning to move. It was only when Molly started to lose her balance, and the dust on the floor began to rise, that Molly realized the *floor* was spinning. Like some kind of eerie fairground ride. The dust rose rank into the parched air, centrifugal force coaxing it into a slow whirlwind.

With a lurching creak the floor stopped rotating. And then, from above, dark shapes began descending creepily into the chamber.

"Holy crud, what are they?" squealed Felicity, shielding her mouth with her arm, her eyes filling with dust.

Skeletons.

Adult-sized, mounted on rusty metal frames that hung from chains. Clothed in threadbare suits and dresses. Their bony hands clutched at where their ears had been; their jaws hung open in screams.

The victims of the Silentman.

Molly heard their screams inside her head now, in place of the ghostly laughter. A chorus of ancient pain. She heard screams *outside* her head, too, as the skeletons halted their descent and began suddenly to swing choppily back and forth on their frames through the dust, gaining speed, while unseen mechanisms whirred above. Molly marvelled at how oddly calm she felt, and she was about to call out some encouraging words to Lowry and Felicity and tell them to try to get back through the door to the tunnel, when she realized that she was screaming her head off.

A round copper plate on the wall was glowing. The fear sensors were well and truly triggered.

Flight of the Swinging Dead

THE SWINGING SKELETONS' HANDS DROPPED from their faces and jerked and flailed as the skeletons span and tilted, rose and plummeted; creaking machinery above was manipulating them like the hands of a mad puppeteer. The bony hand of a dive-bombing skeleton raked across Molly's back, with what looked like long, sharpened metal fingernails. Then Molly saw that the door to the tomb was locking — a complex set of cogs had started moving on a mechanism beneath the handle after the fear sensors had been activated.

"Felicity! Get the door!"

Shrieking, Felicity stumbled across the chamber, tripping over bones, wading into Lowry, who fell wailing to the ground. She wedged the torch under her armpit and tried to access her locksmith's bag. A swinging skeleton whooshed past her. Its claws slashed the bag open. Tools spewed out, and Felicity fell headlong trying to retrieve one. She began to rise …

"Keep down!" Lowry shrieked.

… and a skeleton flew over her head, gambolling upside down on its spinning metal frame, its claws cleaving the dusty air. Felicity sank, choking, to the door, and with a grunt she thrust a randomly chosen tool into the lock mechanism and began to work crudely to crack it.

Her torch fell. Now Felicity was toiling in darkness, the torchlight illuminating the sad scattering of bones across the floor.

Molly heard Lowry cry out as a flying skeleton caught her with its claws. She span around, aiming the camera — she guessed she had four or five shots left on the cartridge — and pushed the button, causing the vault to light up just in time for her to see the same skeleton heading towards her, its grey dress flowing, hands reaching out.

Slow motion.

She saw her own hand held up like that of a traffic warden.

She saw the skeleton hurtling from the gloom, sharpened iron nails foremost.

She saw her own death.

She saw — bizarrely — a vision of herself reaching up to clean the trophies on old Banderfrith's top shelf. She had a sudden mad notion that Banderfrith had given her the job of cleaning his room — of shifting his furniture and stretching to dust high shelves — in order to train her.

To make her stronger.

She stood her ground.

At the last moment, Molly ducked.

The skeleton zipped overhead.

As the skeleton swung back towards her, she reached out and grabbed hold of her bony assailant.

It lofted her into the air like a trapeze. Molly strained to keep hold. She leaned back and pulled her knees up to her chest and struggled to plant her feet on the metal frame holding the skeleton; finding her footing, with groaning effort, she pulled herself upright.

While Felicity wrestled with the door and Lowry screamed and ducked and the hurtling killers carved the dark, Molly scaled the soaring skeleton.

Her feet found the midway bars of the metal frame. Now she was face to face with the skeleton's long-haired skull, which loomed at her through the blackness. She heaved herself higher, one foot disappearing into the ribcage, the other finding a crossbar. Higher she hauled herself, her long-dead dance partner twirling past the other skeletons in a macabre mid-air waltz, until Molly reached the topmost bar of the frame, grabbing hold of the chain that attached the skeleton to the machinery overhead. She felt for the camera, nearly lost balance, aimed it, and pressed the button.

"I've done it!" shouted Felicity — as the camera flash exploded and the chamber turned to pure light, leaving on Molly's retinas the imprint of the complex machinery above her head — and, on the edge of her vision, a skeleton swinging in the direction of Felicity's voice, spinning through space, claws raised. A flying bony food blender on a mission to kill her friend.

With no time to think, Molly reached up and plunged the camera into the machinery above her.

Gears bit it hard. Molly felt like her arm was about to be ripped off. She and her dance partner parted ways on bad terms and at speed. Now Molly was falling through a cyclone of skeletons. She fell into the whorl of bone-dust below and heard a shriek as the skeleton that was heading for Felicity, thrown off course, flew askew and slammed into the wall above Felicity's head.

"Hurry, Molly!" Lowry shouted.

Molly doggy-paddled through the bones, scooping

up the torch. The skeletons, now that the mechanism controlling them was jammed, danced a horrible twitching jig.

Felicity held the door open for Lowry and Molly to go through. Then the girls were squeezing into the narrow corridor, the first people in the history of Howlfair to escape from the tomb housing the victims of the Silentman.

Deal-Breaker

A S SHE CRAWLED ALONG THE PASSAGEWAY, Molly heard a commotion from outside.

Shouting. Orson. Lucinda.

Near the curve in the stairs, Lowry stopped and grabbed her friends. "Wait! I need to say something."

Above ground, Orson Corches could be heard shouting at something to get off him.

"Evans, this isn't the best place for a chat," snapped Felicity. "It's not even the best tomb for a chat."

"Molly, you have to tell the Corcheses you aren't going to do any more corpse-hunting," said Lowry. "It is very flipping obvious to me that whoever hid John Broome's remains definitely didn't want anyone to find them. If the tomb that has the clue to finding John Broome's remains is booby-trapped, imagine what John Broome's actual tomb is like."

263

From outside the tomb came a roar. "The three of you — get out here!"

"Molly, please trust me," said Lowry urgently. "This Silentman business has to end. It's time to break up with the Corcheses. Let me do the talking."

Molly could hear Orson trying to squeeze through the doorway at the top of the steps. "I'm coming in!" he shouted.

Molly chewed her lip. "I need to help the Corcheses so I can save the Excelsior."

Lowry shook her head. "We can save the Excelsior without them."

"I promised my mum."

"And you promised me that you'd start taking me seriously," said Lowry. "I need you to keep your promise. These journalists nearly sent us to our deaths."

"She's right, Thompson," said Felicity. "The Excelsior Guesthouse isn't worth dying for. For all we know, they're working for Benton Furlock."

Orson shouted, "I'm stuck! Lucinda! I'm stuck! Get that blasted cat's teeth off my bum!"

Molly heard a *meow.*

Gabriel.

"Sounds like Gabriel agrees with me and Felicity," said Lowry. She extended a hand that was still shaking wildly from adrenaline. "Come on, Molly Thompson. You've made a deal with the devil, and it's time you cancelled it."

The End

"FLYING SKELETONS!" LUCINDA CRIED, INTERrupting Lowry's vivid account of the misadventure in the tomb. "Orson, would you ever have believed it!"

"Never," Orson grumbled, glaring at Gabriel, who was hissing and squirming in Molly's arms.

"Most regrettable," said Lucinda. "Molly, how could you have blundered into the wrong tomb?" She drew close to Molly, ignoring the hissing cat in the girl's arms. "Did the potion lead you astray?"

"The voices led me to the tomb where the Silentman's victims were buried," said Molly in a low voice, "but the legend was wrong — Broome isn't there. It was a trap."

"So we're no closer to finding Broome's real tomb?"

"There was a clue down there, a clue to finding the tomb," said Molly. "A riddle." She patted the bag around her shoulder. "I've got a photo of it in here.

Thing is, the place was designed to kill anyone who managed to find the clue. That corrupt mayor — or whoever he got to bury John Broome — has a pretty sick sense of humour."

"What about my parents?" blurted Lucinda, stepping back as Gabriel aimed a hiss at her. "Did you see my parents down there? Did they end up murdered by the skeletons? Tell me, Molly — were my parents' corpses in that tomb?"

Molly shook her head. "There were lots of bones on the ground," she said, "but they all looked pretty ancient."

Lucinda sighed. "The tomb of the Silentman still awaits us. My parents may have found it after all."

Again Gabriel hissed. Molly looked over her shoulder at Lowry. The moon came out from behind a caravan of clouds and watched the little group assembled on the hillside.

"Lucinda, I don't want to search for John Broome's grave any more," Molly said.

Lucinda looked aghast.

"You wish to withdraw from our arrangement? After everything my brother and I have done for you? Because of some silly booby-traps?"

"*Silly?*" gasped Molly. "Lucinda, you don't understand — we weren't supposed to come out of that tomb alive! We were nearly chopped to bits by mechanical skeletons with razors for claws. And they were just guarding a flipping *riddle*! Imagine what'll be guarding the crypt that contains Broome's actual remains!"

"Molly, you and your friends just faced a test of courage — *and you passed it*," said Lucinda. "It's time to claim your prize. It's time for us to discover the secret resting place of John Broome."

"Look, Lucinda," said Molly. "Obviously I still really want Howlfair to be in *Country Wonders* magazine..."

Gabriel hissed a loud complaint.

"But also," Molly went on, "we nearly —"

"We nearly just got turned into salami slices by flying skeletons," said Felicity, coming over.

Lowry had approached too. "We don't want you and Orson searching for the Silentman any more," she said. "We don't want you doing any more grave robbing in our town."

Lucinda, her head tilted back so that she was looking at the children down the barrel of her nose, pulled heavy breaths through her nostrils. At last, she spoke. "Orson, take the camera and the bag."

Grunting, Orson shambled over to Molly. He held his hand out and nodded towards the bag. Molly lifted it from her shoulder and handed it to him, glad to be rid of it.

"The camera... I, um, left it in the tomb."

He didn't seem to care. He trudged over to Lucinda, examining the instant photographs in the bag. Molly saw him catch Lucinda's eye and give a brief nod.

"The thing is, she's right, Orson, isn't she?" Lucinda said. "It's horrifying that our lifelong quest to discover the fate of our parents has almost occasioned the deaths of these charming children. It's time we left Howlfair."

Orson mumbled and continued looking at the photographs.

"We release you from your bond, Molly Thompson," Lucinda said. "Thank you — all of you — for your help. We will leave in the morning, and will write a wonderful piece about your town and your guesthouse for *Country Wonders*. Is that acceptable to everyone? Molly?"

To be honest, Molly was finding it hard to believe what she was hearing.

"That sounds ... great."

"And are you all in a fit state to find your own ways home?" Lucinda said sweetly. "I think that Orson and I should go to one of your superb taverns and discuss a possible change of direction for our lives."

"Yes," said Molly. "And ... um, thanks."

"No, thank *you*, Molly," said Lucinda. "I'm truly

sorry that you and your companion were almost murdered by skeletons. My brother and I will see you in the morning and say our goodbyes."

Lucinda nodded at the parked car, and its lights and engine came to life. The driver got out and opened the back doors. The journalists headed to their purring car and Lucinda turned to wave her fingernails at Molly, and then she and her brother vanished into the car and the driver conveyed them away into the night.

Molly realized that the ghost voices had left her head. The potion had worn off.

It was over.

Friend Things

"*S*EE!" LOWRY SAID AS THE GIRLS (AND Gabriel) walked down West Circuit Street, their footfalls echoing in the night-time hush. "Sometimes you just need to be firm with people. We all nearly died — *literally died* — running errands for those creepy journos. Writing a nice article about Howlfair and the Excelsior Guesthouse is the least they can do." She checked her watch. "Holy catfish, I've got to get a wiggle on. My parents'll execute me if they find out I sneaked off. But we'll definitely meet up tomorrow. We've got a lot to discuss."

Still shaken, the girls hurried between the street lamps. Molly turned to Felicity.

"You keep saving my life," she said.

Felicity shrugged and kicked up the low-lying street fog as she walked. "It's a friend thing."

Despite everything, Molly felt a brief flush of happiness.

Meanwhile, sitting in the passenger seat of a car bearing the logo of a consultancy named Abygor and Krool, a cloth bag on his lap, Orson Corches peered at a photograph of a plaque, a photograph Molly had taken in the tomb.

WHERE LIETH THE SILENTMAN?
NOT IN A GRAVEYARD.
BUT RESOLVE MY RIDDLE
AND THOU WILT KNOW:
I FILL AS I EMPTY
I EMPTY AS I FILL
YET NOTHING LEAVETH ME
AND NOTHING ENTERETH.
WHAT AM I?

Secret Guest

APPROACHING THE GUESTHOUSE, MOLLY heard banging and curses coming from the side of the building. Tentatively she approached — and there in the bin area, moonlit, was Gran. She was standing on an upturned bottle crate and tipping rubbish into one of the blue 1,100-litre bins. Just as Molly opened her mouth to call to her, Gran hoisted the rest of her rubbish bag into the bin and scuttled down the side of the guesthouse.

Intrigued, Molly followed.

Stealthily Molly tracked her grandmother through the boot room and through the silent guesthouse.

Up the rear staircase she crept after Gran, ascending the marble steps to the fourth floor.

Gran vanished into a room. Molly tiptoed down

the corridor to find that it wasn't Gran's room —
it was the room next door.

She heard a voice. A man's voice. A *familiar* man's
voice.

Was Gran having a secret fling in the guesthouse?

Now it sounded like she and her guest were
arguing.

She gasped as she realized who it was.

Before she could stop herself, curiosity compelled
Molly to turn the handle. She pushed the door, not
quite expecting it to open.

The room's inhabitants yelped with shock as Molly
tumbled in.

There, by the desk, looking alarmed and packing
a rucksack, was the last werewolf-hunter in Howlfair.

"Gran, I can't believe you've been harbouring a
fugitive!" hissed Molly, gesturing at Wallace Wetherill.
"I mean, it's pretty cool, actually, but —"

"I'm not harbouring him — I'm nursing him,"
said Gran. "Heavy work it is, too. I found him just
after that explosion in the infirmary, the one that he
refuses to tell me anything about, and he was in a
terrible state."

The huge man shook his head and rubbed his side.
"I'm much better now, though," he lied, wincing.

Molly said to Gran, "What do you mean, you *found* him?"

"I'd intended to stay with a friend from the Workers' Union," said Mr Wetherill. "But the friend had left town, and so I …"

"… so he decided to collapse under a tree in the memorial garden on Looking Glass Lane North," said Gran. "I spotted him on my way back from visiting Mrs Considene to discuss the flat."

"I didn't even know you two knew each other," Molly said.

"Oh, we're good buddies, aren't we, Wallace?" said Gran, reaching out to pat his arm. "And it's very good exercise, lugging half-dead six-foot-ten geriatrics around."

"Wait — is this why you've been drinking those pink energy drinks?" asked Molly. "So you can lug Mr Wetherill around?"

"Definitely wasn't for the flavour."

"Your grandmother has nursed me back to fitness — and just in time," said Wetherill. "Benton Furlock's back in town. One of my contacts from the Union spotted him last night."

Molly jolted. "Here? In Howlfair?"

"He was talking to someone on Long Alley, and my friend managed to hide and listen. Furlock's up to some dodgy business at Loonchance Manor at midnight."

"What!"

"Don't worry, Molly — I'm going to catch him."

"Wallace, surely this can wait till your ribs mend?" said Gran.

"No, Sharon," said Wetherill. "This is something that can't wait. Another week might be too late." He sighed. "I didn't mean for that to rhyme."

"But it might be dangerous," said Molly.

"I'm no coward," snapped Wetherill.

Molly was shocked. "I didn't say you were!"

"Well, I've been called one in the past, on account of my being too soft-hearted," he muttered, stretching and pulling on a beanie cap that had been stuffed in his back pocket. *"Trigger-shy coward, caitiff, craven cur…* But tonight I'm going to give Furlock what for."

Molly frowned. She'd recalled how Mr Banderfrith had called Gabriel a *craven caitiff*.

Was it Mr Banderfrith who'd called Mr Wetherill a coward? If so, why, and when?

She opened her mouth to speak, but at that moment, a rumble shook the building.

"What was that?" said Gran, clutching the side of the table.

"I'll go and see," said Molly, turning.

"No!" Wetherill cried. The rumbles turned into shakes. "Stay here. It might be an earthquake."

The walls shivered. Somewhere in the guesthouse, Mrs Hellastroom screamed. The floorboards rattled. The light overhead swung. And then, just as it seemed that the Excelsior might break away from the earth and sail off —

The earthquake ended, to be replaced by the sounds of busy industry: clankings, scrapings, wrenchings, hoistings.

Gingerly Molly guided Gran to the bed and sat her down.

"Stay here," Molly ordered Gran and Mr Wetherill, heading to the door before either adult could stop her. "I'm going to find out what's going on."

A Reversal of Furnishings

THE CORRIDOR WAS FULL OF A&K STAFF IN their hats and sunglasses. Dozens of them. They were pulling the oval portraits from the walls and throwing them into boxes. They were stripping the paint from the walls and pulling up the polished floorboards with crowbars and rolling out the previous drab carpets. The lights flickered.

"What are you doing?" Molly shouted, running up to one, then another.

They ignored her.

From downstairs, Molly heard her mother scream.

Molly ran.

The staircase was no longer jade with a golden bannister; it was dusty and rickety, as before. Suited workers were wrenching down the last of the hanging vines and hoisting the funeral urns from their carved alcoves.

Down in the lobby, Mum was gaping in horror at where the gigantic chandelier had hung only a few minutes earlier.

Hordes of removals workers were carting slabs of marble ripped from the floor; workers on ladders removed the ceiling beams. The stone ravens had flown.

"What's going on?" Mum cried, grabbing at workers. They shrugged her off. "What are you doing to my guesthouse? Where have all the guests gone?" She span around. "Molly — did you do this?"

Mum's words stung Molly. "I don't know what's going on!"

Then she spied something on the guestbook table. A small jewellery box.

"Molly, what's happening? Tell me! Wait — did *I* upset the Corcheses? Where have they gone?"

Ignoring her wailing mother, Molly blundered through the crowd of crate-lugging workers to the table and examined the box. It was the box in which Lucinda had kept a white worm. She lifted it carefully.

"Molly Thompson, if you're not going to answer me, I'm going to look for the Corcheses myself!" Mum shouted, heading to her office to get her coat.

Her words were lost on Molly. The sound of someone thundering down the stairs was also lost on Molly. She was transfixed by the box.

She had to open it.

Bracing herself, she flipped open the lid as her mother ran from the guesthouse into the night, dropping her car keys twice on the way.

There was a note inside the jewellery box.

"Molly, I don't know what's going on, but I've got to go," said a gruff voice behind her. It was Mr Wetherill in his beanie hat, lumbering along with a rucksack on his huge back, the straps straining. "I can't miss my chance to catch that fink Furlock sneaking back into his old headquarters at Loonchance Manor after we banished him. You can't follow me. I've locked your grandmother in my room, so you'll need to go up and free her once I've gone."

Molly didn't even hear him. She was looking at the note — and realizing what she'd done.

"Oh no…"

Dear Molly,

We have found the Crypt of the Blue Moon, the burial place of John Broome, the place where his greatest treasure is to be found.

The treasure? Oh, not his silly magical bell.

280

The treasure locked in Broome's tomb is his own ghost! THE SILENTMAN. The phantom, you see, was never trapped in a snuffbox and thrown into a stream. The silentman has been waiting centuries in a secret crypt for someone to find and release him, in fulfilment of a certain old prophecy.

How hilarious that you never suspected that the silentman was the monster in Wendell Zoet's prophecy! You might have discovered it, had all the books about the silentman not been removed from Howlfair Library...

Anyway, dear Molly: at midnight I will lead my brother into the crypt and set the silentman free, bringing the Dark Days back to Howlfair.

Thank you for your help!

Lucinda x

Trust

LUCKILY, THE OFFICE, UNTOUCHED BY THE Excelsior's recent makeover, was now empty of renovators. Molly was relieved to discover that the telephone hadn't been cut off. She called Lowry's house, praying that someone, preferably Lowry, would answer at this late hour.

Her sister answered.

"Frances! I'm sorry to call so late," she babbled. "I've got a really, really urgent question for Lowry and it's literally life or death, and —"

"Lowry!" shouted Frances, having walked away from the phone as soon as she heard Molly wittering.

Molly heard Mrs Evans telling Lowry off for having inconsiderate friends who call late.

"Molly?" Lowry answered. "Why are you calling? I'm already grounded for sneaking out."

"Lowry, listen to me — Lucinda and Orson have

found out where John Broome is buried, and it's the Crypt of the Blue Moon! The Silentman is the monster in that prophecy! But I didn't know it because Lucinda and Orson must have taken all the books about the Silentman story out of the library, and also the phantom *isn't* trapped in a snuffbox at the bottom of the Six Bridges Stream — he's trapped in the crypt, waiting to be released by a girl or a woman leading a man or a boy at midnight! And I don't know why, but Lucinda's going to lead Orson into the crypt and let the Silentman out, which will trigger the prophecy and bring the Dark Days back to Howlfair, and I think they might be working for Furlock!"

There was a long pause. "Lowry, say something!"

"Sorry — I'm trying to choose between several words that accurately express my feelings that you've brought about the end of Howlfair and probably the end of the world. I'll go with 'botheration'."

"Lowry! Can you please take this seriously?"

"I am taking it seriously. We need to find the Crypt of the Blue Moon and stop the Corcheses from fulfilling the prophecy. So you need to figure out that riddle that you found in the tomb. What was it? Something about filling and emptying…"

Molly said, *"I fill as I empty, I empty as I fill, but nothing leaves me and nothing enters — what am I?"*

"That's the one. Think you can solve it?"

"Course I can flipping solve it," said Molly. She stared at the ceiling for two seconds. *"An hourglass."*

"Like an egg timer thing?" said Lowry.

"Yes, an egg timer thing. Because the top bit empties and the bottom bit fills with sand, but the sand never leaves."

"Ah, I see!" said Lowry. "Jeepers, Thompson, you're good."

"I know," said Molly. "But it doesn't help us find the Crypt of the Blue Moon, does it? Unless the Crypt of the Blue Moon is literally an hourglass. Which is unlikely. So basically…"

"So basically we need to get Carl," said Lowry. "We need his burial records and his amazing knowledge of graves."

Molly flinched. "You want me to get help finding a crypt — from the guy who nearly killed me in a crypt?"

In a small voice, Lowry said, "Molly, you're going to have to start trusting Carl at some point."

Molly sighed. She nodded.

"Are you still there?" Lowry asked.

"I'm nodding."

"Of course you are. Remind me, when all this is over, to explain to you how telephones work. In the meantime: where's Carl?"

"I don't know!"

"Stop being ridiculous. You're Molly Thompson. You can figure anything out."

A thought came to Molly's mind: *What does Carl want most in the world?*

"Protection," she muttered to herself.

"What?" said Lowry.

"I'm thinking aloud."

"About..."

"About how the thing Carl wants more than anything else is to feel safe. So he'll have gone somewhere familiar. And he wants somewhere that feels like home..."

"He still has that teddy bear his parents gave him," said Lowry.

"Yeah. And he's a creature of habit and routine. And he has some lock-picking skills he learned from Felicity — he'd probably use them to get into a secure hiding place, somewhere that gives him comfort, but which the bullies can't get into."

"Maybe he's hiding in a tomb? In a graveyard," said Lowry.

"Sorry, contestant number one — a graveyard is not comforting or homelike."

"Loonchance Manor?"

"Loonchance Manor probably has ghouls in it."

"So where is he?"

Molly closed her eyes tightly. *"Wetherill's Store,"* she said. "He broke in. He knows nobody will expect him to be there because it's a crime scene. There are plenty of rooms he can hide in, and an exit at the back, leading to an alley." She paused for a breath. "Lowry?"

"I'm nodding," said Lowry. "So — you know what you have to do now?"

"I have to get Carl to help me find the Crypt of the Blue Moon and somehow stop the Corcheses setting a madness-making phantom loose in Howlfair and bringing back the Dark Days."

Lowry tutted. "I mean *before* that, silly."

Molly frowned. "In case you're wondering," she said, "I'm frowning."

"Molly, you have to trust Carl."

Crime Scene

"*C*ARL? ARE YOU IN THERE?"

Molly peered, her face framed by her hands, through the window of Mr Wetherill's Weaponry Store, trying to see any sign of life beyond the rows of fake stakes, boxes of silver bullets and plastic harpoon muskets. A police seal on the door read:

CRIME SCENE — DO NOT ENTER

Nobody, it seemed, had tampered with the seal. Molly headed for a nearby alley filled with bins, spent too much time painfully climbing a wall, and arrived in the narrower alley to the rear of the shop.

She counted her way along the row of back doors. Found the right one. Crouched by the door and hissed through the keyhole: "Carl!"

She waited. Nothing.

"Carl! It's Molly!" She wasn't sure what to say. "Danger is afoot!"

That sounded stupid. But it sounded less stupid than trying to sound like an owl, which was the secret signal with which she'd once agreed to summon him, before the incident in Loonchance Manor.

She waited.

Still nothing.

She sighed, annoyed.

"Twit-twoo!" she sang through the keyhole.

This time she heard a smothered laugh.

"Yeah, hilarious," she hissed. "Open up, Carl, it's urgent!"

She heard Carl approaching the door.

"How did you know I'd be here?" he whispered through the keyhole.

"I just figured out you were here, OK? Because I know you."

Silence. "Really?"

"Just flipping open up, Grobman."

Moments later he opened the door, dressed in one of Mr Wetherill's old coats. A chilly corridor filled with Wallace's boxes of books — upturned, their contents spilled — stretched behind him.

"I was just coming to see you," Carl said, his dark eyes animated. "I need your help with something."

"It'll have to wait, Carl," said Molly. "The Corcheses... They're going to open John Broome's tomb at midnight — it turns out that the Silentman is the monster in an old prophecy about the Crypt of the Blue Moon, and if the Corcheses let him out of his crypt at midnight, the Dark Days will come back..." She looked at her watch. "So we need to find out where the Silentman is buried *before midnight*..."

"I think you'd better come inside," Carl said.

"Carl, no! We don't have time! We need to break into St Fell's Church and get those burial records by midnight!"

"Follow me," he said. "I've got them already."

Stars

"CRIPES — THE POLICE REALLY TRASHED THE place," said Molly, stepping over a broken stepladder as Carl led her through the dark corridor to Mr Wetherill's study.

"One of the problems with living in a crime scene is that you're not allowed to do any tidying up," said Carl. "On the plus side ... you never have to tidy up."

He opened the study door. In the cramped, lamp-lit room, which looked as though a minor cyclone had ripped a thousand books from the ancient shelves, Carl had spread out numerous old scrolls, maps, charts and diagrams. Broken glass was everywhere. Mr Wetherill's old chair had been snapped into pieces, the seat cut open by the police in case there'd been a weapon sewn into it. Open records books and scribbled notes obscured a desk.

"These are photocopies of everything I thought

might help — death records, burial locations, maps," said Carl, gesturing at the floor and the desk. "I've been trying to find out where John Broome's buried." He looked bashful. "I wanted to figure it out so I could help you with your mission and prove to you that I'm good for something. But I've been looking at the records for hours and I'm not getting anywhere."

"You just need to know how to put the clues together — like you're doing a jigsaw."

Molly rolled up her sleeves. They slipped back down. She pushed aside some books and sat on the floorboards.

"Tonight I found a riddle that gives a clue about where the secret tomb is," she said. "Orson and Lucinda have the riddle too, and they must've used it to find the Silentman."

"What's the riddle?"

"*I fill as I empty, I empty as I fill, but nothing leaves me and nothing enters — what am I? And the answer is...*"

"A teacup!" said Carl. "No, wait. Lungs! No, wait..."

"Carl, I've already solved it. The answer is *an hourglass.*" Carl looked blank.

"Just take my word for it," said Molly. "Thing is, I don't know how that helps us."

Carl said, "I do."

"Really?"

Sweeping some stacks of manila envelopes aside, he lifted a huge, heavy book from beside the desk, blew the dust from its parched cover as though blowing a dandelion clock, and flipped through the pages.

"This is the book with the complete list of burial sites in Howlfair. There are names of people buried, in alphabetical order, and the locations — but some entries don't have actual locations, just little symbols." He stopped flipping and pointed at random to a name and a symbol. The pages were crowded with such entries. "Maybe the hourglass is one of the symbols. But it'd take a year to go through every entry looking for an hourglass."

He handed Molly the book. She moved through the pages, scrutinizing the information.

"You're right. It'd take too long."

"So how do we find out what the hourglass means?"

"Well, we know it's the symbol for some sort of building, because the entries without symbols all list buildings," said Molly. "I reckon the symbols stand for private residences, special locations, monuments. Like…" She slapped her head. "Flipping heck, I'm so stupid! No wonder the Corcheses solved it so easily. Carl — it's Kroglin Mausoleum!"

Carl looked blank.

"Above the door to Kroglin Mausoleum is the

292

family crest of arms, and it has an hourglass in it. That's where John Broome is buried! That's where the Crypt of the Blue Moon is. That's where the Corches have gone to let the Silentman loose."

"So what do we do?" said Carl, fretting.

"We get up and go there and stop them!" growled Molly. She struggled to rise. Her legs felt wobbly. She tried to push herself to her feet and fell sideways.

"Molly? Are you OK? What are you doing?"

She righted herself. "I'm trying to flipping get up."

"Then why aren't you, you know, um, getting up? Are you hurt?"

Molly fell forward. She pushed herself upright with huge effort. Her heart felt like a furious woodpecker hammering its beak into the trunk of her spine. She discovered that she was having difficulty breathing.

"Molly, what's wrong?"

It was no good — the thought of leaving the shop and heading off to yet another evil crypt with Carl Grobman had sent her into a full panic. Especially since she had no plan for apprehending the Corcheses.

"I'm scared," she said at last.

Carl looked confused. "Of course you're scared. Especially after what happened in the summer. When I — when I betrayed you." He rose to his feet. "And when you risked your life and rescued me from the ghouls I'd helped set on you. But listen — I'm on your side now." He shook his head. "How can I convince you I've changed?"

Molly didn't know. All she knew was that her body wasn't letting her go with Carl to another tomb.

"You can't," she said.

Carl blinked away tears. "Molly, listen. What I did to you, it's in my head all the time. The shame of it. It's like — you know those dreams I used to have, where Lady Orgella ..."

Molly winced at the name.

"... where her mouth would go huge and she'd breathe me into it and I'd go into the darkness? I don't have those dreams any more."

"Really?"

"No. Now it's like I'm in the darkness all the time."

Molly looked down. She'd had the same nightmare — just once — of the vile demoness with the vacuum breath, sucking her into Hell. In her dream, her dad had appeared and saved her, giving Lady Orgella a good sock to the jaw. But Carl —

Carl had never known his dad. Or his mum. He'd spent his life with nobody but an evil demonworshipper to protect him: Benton Furlock, who'd branded him with the mark of Lady Orgella, and who'd promised to keep him safe if he'd do Furlock's bidding.

"Molly," Carl said, his despondent eyes betraying a spark of what? Hope? "Underneath Loonchance Manor ... when I saw you coming back through that door, and you shouted at the ghouls to leave me alone... I'd never seen real goodness before that moment. Before you came through the door, I'd accepted I was going to die, and I knew I deserved it. The sight of you in that doorway was the most amazing thing I've ever seen in the whole world. What you did — it was more beautiful than..." He flailed for words. "Than the stars. Because you didn't even have to do it! You didn't *want* to do it. You weren't some daring adventurer who rescues twelve people before breakfast. You were just ... *you*."

He turned away. He slid something out from underneath a pile of papers. He turned back. He gave it to Molly.

Molly was holding a framed photograph.

"This might help you to not be scared," said Carl. "Of me, of the Corcheses, of the Silentman — of anything."

Slowly Molly rose to her feet.

"Unlike me, you've got a past to be proud of," Carl said. "And a past you don't even know about."

Secret Weapon

THE FRAME WAS CRACKED, THE PICTURE ripped and water-damaged. She did not see, under a crease, the smudged image of Benton Furlock. But she could make out some of the other people pictured.

"The Guild of Asphodel," said Carl. "I've been reading about it in Wetherill's notebooks. Citizens of Howlfair who tried to find out if there were monsters in our valley. They took their name from an old guild of miners who guarded the gateway to Hell. Look — there's Mr Wetherill with his muskets! And — would you believe it? — Mrs de Ville! With a ghoul-killing litter-picker. Mr Banderfrith with his sword-stick..."

"Banderfrith? No way!"

"There's Farmer Digby with a harpoon gun. And a bunch of people in the background who I can't quite make out. And right in the middle..."

Molly was trying, and failing, to blink away her amazement.

Her confusion.

"Dad ..." She felt weak. Dizzy. "... *and me.*"

Her dad was standing in the middle of the group, grinning his boyish grin, holding a curly haired baby girl.

"You look just like him," said Carl. "And do you notice something? Everyone else has a weapon, don't they? And your dad..."

"He doesn't have a weapon."

Carl shook his head. "Course he does."

Molly looked up with a frown.

"*You're* the weapon," said Carl. "Somehow he knew it'd be you who'd save this town."

Molly struggled to breathe. "But I don't know how!"

"*You don't have to,*" said Carl firmly. "You're the *weapon*, Molly. The weapon doesn't need to know how to fight. It just has to let someone take hold of it."

Her face was an embarrassing wet mess and her nose was running. She raked the back of her hand across her face.

"Who? Who, Carl? My dad's dead!"

"He's part of something bigger, Molly. I don't know what, exactly. Fate? Destiny? Some invisible gang of spirits looking after our town? The forces of goodness?" He threw his hands up. "It doesn't matter! What matters is what you are. And what you are is…"

Molly watched Carl grasp for the right words.

"You're the secret weapon of the Guild of Asphodel. You're the one the demons never saw coming. Wherever the monsters are, somehow you'll show up too." He straightened. "And so will I. I promise. Just give me a chance."

Molly stared at her dad's delighted, proud face. Then her eyes refocused, and she saw her own face reflected in the broken glass in the frame. It was the face of a scared girl who liked to sit at home solving puzzles. A girl with a quick mind and permanently frayed nerves. A girl who could outsmart ghouls and demons. A girl who could forgive.

The secret weapon of the Guild of Asphodel.

"Flipping Nora."

Within the minute, in her beaten-up plimsolls and frayed jeans and her *Doris de Ville's Street Cleaning Crew* tee-shirt, Molly Thompson was dashing after Carl Grobman through the night, towards the Crypt of the Blue Moon.

She had no plan whatsoever.

But she knew that she had to stop the journalists

from opening the tomb of the Silentman. Because if the Dark Days returned to a town wholly unprepared for monsters, Howlfair would fall, and quickly. And Molly knew better than anyone what would happen if Howlfair fell — because earlier that year she'd deciphered the obscure wording on Howlfair's flag and discovered the town's ancient motto:

If Howlfair falls, the whole world falls.

A Trapdoor

EMERGING FROM THE BELT OF TREES, MOLLY looked up at the silver wolf at the top of the mausoleum's dome. Below the Kroglin family crest — the hourglass through which tiny stars trickled, with a sleeping wolf beneath it — the door to the mausoleum was ajar, broken, hanging from its hinges.

"They've already got in," said Molly. "If Lucinda's led Orson into the crypt, they've already fulfilled half the prophecy — and if they free the Silentman, then the other half is fulfilled." She stamped her foot. "We need a flipping plan!"

"Did you have a plan when you came to rescue me under Loonchance Manor?"

"No," said Molly. "I just winged it."

"Then I think we should wing it."

Inside, the same paint-splattered sheets lay scattered over the mosaic floor. The scaffolding was

300

the same. The pearly dome overhead glowed with moonlight as before.

But the great circular trapdoor leading to the underground crypt was open. Torn rags of unworldly moss hung from its uprighted iron edge. Spores of putrefaction dallied above the black gaping mouth of the entrance to the mausoleum.

"Oh, crud!" said Molly. "We're too late — Lucinda's led Orson into the crypt!"

Molly ran, Carl following. Without thinking, she reached a hand behind her, like a relay racer, and Carl grabbed it as they approached the open trapdoor.

They descended into the gloom, stumbling down a stone staircase. Then Molly heard a muted laugh and looked up to see a small, pale hand push the trapdoor shut.

A Trap

DARKNESS.

A darkness so sudden and profound that it felt to Molly as though it had rugby-tackled her. Her senses grasped for meaning. Her mind emptied of useful information and swelled with panic. And then —

Light! A pulsing sting of blue light from above — it took Molly a few moments to realize that the window hatch on the trapdoor had been slid open and a face — no, two faces — no, three faces — were looming on the other side of the blue, hazy, ancient glass.

On the left: Lucinda Corches.

On the right: Lucinda's ghastly brother.

And the face in the middle, dread — pale, hollow-cheeked, with a horn-like, drooping moustache — belonged to Benton Furlock.

"I say, Molly Thompson," said Furlock, his viperish voice muted by the azure glass. "It rather looks like you've just led a boy into the Crypt of the Blue Moon. At midnight. Isn't there some sort of old prophecy about that?"

Molly's eyes flickered towards the Corcheses. They'd been working for Furlock all along.

A grin opened on Furlock's face like an earthquake crack.

"Oh, how rude of me!" he said, turning to Lucinda, then to Orson, then back to Molly. "Allow me to introduce the ghouls who've been staying in your guesthouse."

The Whispering Heart

"IT DELIGHTS ME," SAID FURLOCK, "THAT NOSY, know-it-all Molly Thompson had *no idea* that two ghouls have been impersonating Lucinda and Orson Corches all week."

Molly felt faint with shame and horror.

"All week! Encouraging you to sneak into the ghoul-proofed tomb that they themselves could not enter; to crawl through a tunnel only a child could squeeze through; to get the clue they needed to find John Broome's tomb! To discover the secret resting place of the Silentman — the Crypt of the Blue Moon!" Furlock laughed deliriously, his moustache swaying hypnotically. "Of course, my ghouls could not have fulfilled Zoet's prophecy themselves — because they are not a man and a woman, merely demonic corpse eaters *impersonating* a man and a woman! Did you not suspect anything?"

Molly said nothing. In her heart she knew she'd suspected something all along. But she'd been so desperate to save the Excelsior that she'd pushed aside her unease. Now she could see her face, its reflection dimly superimposed over Furlock's, on the blue glass above her, and it was glowing with humiliation.

Furlock shrugged. "Well, before I let you know of your fate," he went on, "I must say how amusing it is to see young Mr Grobman again! Once more you've helped lure Molly Thompson into a trap."

"Don't listen to him," Carl said to Molly. "I wasn't helping him this time. I'll *never* help him."

"I know," coughed Molly. She could barely speak for fear. She eyed the ghoulish Lucinda and Orson with disbelief. "I don't know anything else right now, but I know *that*."

Furlock gaped with grim delight. "Oh, Grobman didn't help *me* lure you into this trap, Molly! He helped you lure *yourself*!"

Molly frowned. "What?"

"All *I* did was leave a book — *Prophecies of Certain Doom* by Yehudi Mantle — on a shelf of Howlfair Library where I knew you'd find it," Furlock said, mock innocently, showing his slab-like teeth. "I gave you a prophecy — a recipe for bringing back the Dark Days — and then I commissioned two of my ghouls —

305

Lady Orgella herself commanded the ghouls to return to my service — to pose as journalists and engage you in a hunt for a tomb. Through my research I had already discovered that the Silentman was the monster in Wendell Zoet's prophecy..." — Molly recalled now how the library had been emptied of books about John Broome and the Silentman story — "but *your own soul*, Molly Thompson, led you to bring Carl here in fulfilment of that prophecy." He turned his gaze to the boy. "You see, Carl, deep down, Molly Thompson *wants* the Dark Days to return."

"I flipping do not!" Molly protested.

"Of course you do, brat! One only has to see how your grubby little face lights up when you speak of Howlfair's legends. You long to be a part of the thrilling stories you read in the history books. You feel that people would *listen* to you if they knew the monsters were real. They would take you seriously. You feel that hellish perils would call forth some inner heroism in you — some trace of your father's lineage — that remains untapped in these tawdry times."

Molly's face stiffened. "Don't talk about my dad."

Furlock merely smirked. The light behind him, it seemed to Molly, began to change, swelling as it pressed through the window's blue glass. Suddenly the straggles of moss dangling around Molly began to twitch, to move towards the light, to coil delightedly. "Do you think your father would be proud of you, Molly?" he sneered. "Oh, what challenges you and your friends overcame to seal his beloved town's doom!"

"I didn't mean to!" Molly cried.

"Lady Orgella knew what you would do," Furlock snapped, and Molly flinched at the sound of that name. "The Mistress of Ghouls told me that your wicked little soul would lead you to fulfil the prophecy. You are doomed to do my mistress's bidding, Molly Thompson. I have the honour of serving her freely — but you, Molly, you have no choice."

Molly turned from the window, shaking. The stone step below her feet seemed washed with the spangly cyan light filtering from the window. All around her, dangling locks of moss and ferny fronds writhed in the blue light.

What if Furlock was right?

What if Molly really did, secretly, long to live in the Howlfair of old? Back when monsters and citizens warred and the night sky rang with the gorgeous voices of werewolves and vampires peered through frosty windows...

She remembered what Felicity had said, only days ago, and which Lady Orgella had said in her dream:

I reckon Molly secretly wants the Dark Days to come back.

307

She wobbled on the step. Carl grabbed her shoulder to steady her.

"I do have a flipping choice," she said at last, pulling away from Carl's grip. Unsteadily she began to descend into the gloom, blue-tinted coils of flora unwinding, reaching out to caress her.

"Where are you going?" said Carl.

"I'm going to find us a way out of here. And I'm not going set the Silentman free. I'm not going to fulfil that prophecy."

"But Molly, you've already fulfilled it!" called Furlock, and Molly heard the vile laughter of the ghouls impersonating Lucinda and Orson Corches. "You've led Carl into the Crypt of the Blue Moon at midnight. So now *the undead thing within will quit his slumber and call forth all those as hellish as he, till the Dark Days return.* A prophecy cannot be cancelled!"

Molly stopped. The ghoulish laughter enveloped her.

"But there's some good news, Molly!" Furlock said. "A secret tunnel down there leads to the grounds of the town hall. You and Grobman might find it and escape before the phantom can find you. But make no mistake: the Silentman will rise and leave this crypt, and he will ring a fiery bell and waken every fiend as hellish as he, and the final darkening of Howlfair will begin."

Last Words

MOLLY LOOKED DOWN AT THE GLOOMY steps that fell spiralling into the abysmal crypts below. As the blue light swelled and the underground flora unfurled, Molly thought she saw, at the bottom of the steps, the outline of an iron gate, like you'd find at the entrance to a grand manor. She imagined John Broome, the Silentman, sealed in a vault somewhere in the blackness beyond the gateway.

"We must be off," Furlock called through the glass. "Even my ghouls don't fancy sticking around when a phantom made of pure hatred rises. And I have a meeting with Wallace Wetherill."

Molly looked up, frowning.

"Mr Wetherill knows you're in town," she babbled before Furlock could turn away. She hated the way fear was making her voice warble. "He's looking for you. He probably followed you here."

Furlock moved his white face closer to the glass, and he withdrew from inside his jacket his sinister crystal hand. His breath spread, freezing over the glass. He rested the fingers on the window.

"Mr Wetherill only knows I'm in town because I staged a number of encounters with his ever-so-subtle scouts from the Workers' Union. Presently he's heading to Loonchance Manor, where he'll spend half an hour searching for me. I aim to show up in time to let him think he found me."

"What for?" called Molly. "What are you going to do to him?"

"I'm going to let him see for himself that Lucinda and Orson Corches are ghouls. So he can try to kill them."

To his right and his left, the ghoul-journalists' grinning faces began to transform.

The heads elongated hideously. The foreheads shrank away and the lower jaws hinged open. The eyes bulged. The skin became dead and the hair turned white. Lucinda's already hefty teeth became twisted, brown fangs; Orson's already hollow eye sockets became craters.

Molly and Carl clutched each other.

"You ... want him to kill them?" Molly stammered.

"Oh, no, Molly. The ghouls will flee before

Wetherill can summon the courage to aim those silly weapons he's been carrying. They will pass through the room where the *real* Lucinda and Orson Corches are waiting, hypnotized…"

"The real Lucinda and Orson?"

"The *real* journalists are here in Howlfair. They've been here all along — I diverted them as soon as they arrived. They are under the spell of very dark magic. I have programmed them to leap out at dear Wallace as he blunders after the real ghouls. In a touching display of long-overdue bravery, Wetherill will blow two innocent people to smithereens. Meanwhile, I will have left the manor and one of my ghouls will have placed an urgent call to our chief of police, describing how Wallace Wetherill chased two journalists into Loonchance Manor with a pair of muskets. The bodies will be found. Wetherill will be arrested for murder. Discredited, his slanderous words against me will be called into question, and I will return to Howlfair just in time for our current mayor to … disappear. I will become the new mayor, and my plans for Howlfair — Lady Orgella's plans for Howlfair — will unfold."

He held up his sinister crystal hand; the light above him, which Molly now saw was pulsing from a moon that was shrugging off a gown of cloud, lit it like a macabre lantern. The ghouls moved away from the window, heading off on their awful mission.

Furlock said, *"Good night, Molly Thompson."*

Momentarily Molly struggled to think of something to say before Furlock left. She felt as though, on top of letting him lock her and Carl in a crypt, letting the vile demon-worshipper have the last word was an indignity too far. But she could conjure no words worth saying. Her mouth gaped helplessly. And then, as Furlock began to turn to follow his ghouls, Carl Grobman raced to the top step and slammed both palms against the glass, making Furlock turn with a look of alarm.

"You think you're about to win, don't you, Furlock?"

The grey face smirked. "I think I've already won, you worthless orphan," Furlock said. "What do *you* think?"

"I think," said Carl, "that you're about to find out what the secret weapon of the Guild of Asphodel is capable of."

Then Molly felt Carl grab her hand as he trotted down the cold steps.

"What are we doing?" Molly whispered.

"We're going to try to escape, and we're probably going to run into the Silentman," said Carl. Molly could tell he was trying hard to sound tough and brave. But there was a wild waver to his voice, a sob of terror waiting to pounce from behind the veil of his words. "And you're going to show me what you're made of." He coughed. "Hopefully."

Molly glanced over her shoulder. As Furlock headed away, the clouds above the dome of the Kroglin Mausoleum headed away too, as if to accompany Furlock on his mission; and moonlight, somehow marvellously concentrated as it pressed through the crystal of the dome, pierced the blue glass of the trapdoor window. It lavished the crypt — the steps, the walls, the depths that dangled like doom in the gloom below Molly and Carl — with blue lunar lustre.

It revealed a sight that caused Molly's wits to scatter like skittles.

Boom

"FLIPPING NORA."

Stone staircases plummeted and coiled and led to scores of burial vaults with ghastly carvings on the doors — skeletons and hooded figures, demons and wolves — and in the moonlight, ethereal flowers and vines and ferns furled and unfurled and luxuriated, almost humming with delight. At the bottom of the steps was a wrought iron gateway, and the flora curled to form lettering over the gate:

The Crypt of the Blue Moon

The children descended. Now Molly noticed that the air was filled with weird echoes that formed a single, solid voice, like the chanted note of a hooded monk reverberating in a black cathedral.

They reached the gates. Shakily Carl pulled them open, and Molly followed him through to a circular platform, overseen by the statue of a wolf, mid-snarl, standing on its rear legs and reaching for the children with its claws. The blue moonlight made the ancient moss and cobwebs glow. Further staircases led to crypts; one led down to the lower levels.

"Let's hurry," Molly whispered, nodding towards the staircase. But the children had barely made it to the top step when suddenly, from the depths, a boom rocked the tomb.

Something had broken free.

Red dust surged from the crypts below. The stairs shook, sending Molly and Carl tumbling down. Winded, her hipbones and elbows and knees and head clunking off the spinning steps, Molly screeched and cradled her skull. All Carl's bravery fled and now he was screaming. The world was revolving. Scarlet dust whirled in the hurtling darkness. Molly grabbed the frozen edge of a step but felt herself fall away from Carl. Her terror was like a plunge through a crack in polar ice: electrifying, heart-stopping, total. Then a space cleared in the dust cloud below her as though an unseen mouth had sucked the dust away, and Molly thought she saw, on a staircase below, a floating shape ascending, something formed from fury, whose touch was madness —

The Silentman.

The Silent Scream

A ND SUDDENLY SHE FOUND HERSELF OUT-side.

It was bright.

Molly blinked, shielded her eyes.

What was happening?

She was on a park bench with her dad. They were sitting in the sun, reading library books. Years ago.

"Dad?"

He snorted and held up his book. "What tosh!" he said.

Molly saw her hands lower her own book. As the memory took over, she felt her mouth say: "Tosh, Dad?"

He turned the book so she could see the title:

The Scream of the Silentman
Legend, History and Prophecy

"There's this chap, John Broome, who supposedly becomes a really evil phantom," Dad said. "But it doesn't make sense. He wasn't evil — he was a hero! He used to stand in our Dance Square every morning, reading out the daily notices to the townsfolk, and he'd always make a point of voicing the concerns of poor people and orphans and widows. He saved Howlfair from an army of phantoms, and this crooked mayor set him up and executed him. And then suddenly he's a phantom, and he's supposed to become evil and start killing people?" He blew a raspberry, which made Molly giggle. "No way, Moll. Good people don't just stop being good, unless they were faking it to start with. And this guy wasn't faking it. He was... He was like..."

Dad stared up at the clouds and lifted a hand as though to pluck an imaginary apple from a tree. Mum called it his Shakespeare pose.

"He was like ... a voice of the voiceless. And the poor geezer ended up a ghost with no voice of his own, just a silent scream inside his mind. He had no way of being heard, no way of letting out the pain of being betrayed. Can you imagine how lonely that must feel?"

The sky suddenly darkened. Molly looked up to see the clouds turning red and knitting together. The memory was dissolving. She looked back at her dad, and he was growing faint. Now she could hear Carl's voice. She'd never heard a more terrified voice.

"Molly!"

A voice of the voiceless…

"Molly — he's coming for us!"

The vision was gone and Molly was in the Crypt of the Blue Moon again. She looked down and saw that the Silentman was on the staircase.

The phantom reached out a hand in its trailing sleeve as he climbed the gloomy steps, clenching and unclenching his fingers slowly, as though underwater.

His town crier's hat obscured his face.

In his other hand was a flaming crier's bell, furnace red, as though plucked from a blacksmith's forge, streaming fire and thick smoke. His robe flowed in unseen currents. Then he tilted back his head, and Molly's stomach lurched as she saw the cracked face. The eyes were swollen with fury. Across his mouth was fixed the cruel metal gag. Molly saw the deep welt around his neck from where he'd been hanged. She knew that the moment he took hold of her, she'd hear, in her own head, his eternal internal scream of rage and betrayal and loneliness.

A voice of the voiceless …

"Molly!" Carl, above her, screamed. "Molly, what are we going to do?"

She shut her eyes. There was only one thing she could think to do. She just didn't know whether it was the right thing.

She ran down the steps, towards the Silentman. She reached out her hand.

… poor geezer ended up without a voice…

"Molly! Molly, what are you doing?"

The Silentman drew close. His spectral fingers took hold of Molly's, and he dragged her down into the rumbling dark.

Broome

THIS WAS THE MADNESS THAT HIS VICTIMS had known: the sound of the scream once trapped in the Silentman's mind, a scream that could never get free.

Now the sound was in Molly's mind too. Not just a sound, playing in the auditorium of her skull; the inner scream seemed to Molly like a whole universe. Simple, infinite, absolute.

She felt her thoughts dissolve like a fizzy tablet in water.

Her memories disintegrated.

... *voice of the voiceless* ...

... *poor geezer ended up without a voice* ...

... *voice of the* ...

... *ended up without a voice* ...

... *the voiceless* ...

... *poor geezer ended* ...

… voiceless …

At last the scream overwhelmed her.

She felt the aimless supernova rage of John Broome, a pain he could never express, the supreme sadness of his betrayal. All other thoughts vanished; all but one, which she clung to: the thought of her father in Ablemarch's Department Store.

The thought of how he'd stopped a fight from breaking out by just *listening*.

With all her strength she forced herself to listen. To discern the different strands of the Silentman's pain.

And suddenly she knew that the Silentman didn't want to drive her mad. He wanted a voice. He wanted to let out his scream.

In a moment of insanity or wisdom, Molly opened her mouth wide.

And although the Silentman's trapped scream seemed too huge, too cosmic to squeeze through a childish soul as slender as hers, she let his scream surge through her windpipe. She lent the Silentman her voice. Immediately she felt as though lava were flowing through her; she thought the pressure of the scream would cause her to explode. She ran out of air. Her lungs compressed, collapsed, and then something unexpected and alarming happened: she began to hear *words* writhing in the scream. A human voice —

Suddenly the scream ended. Everything was terrifyingly peaceful. Was it the peace of death? Molly did not know. She felt nowhere. Then she saw a light. A silvery light. A form, a shape, a person, materializing.

John Broome.

Voice of the Voiceless

BUT HE NO LONGER WORE THE METAL GAG. He was a shimmering shape, a human blue-print made of starlight, decked in his town crier's garb. And the bell in his hand no longer bled fire. It gave off light. It wasn't a bell that would summon evil; it was the bell it had once been, the bell that had banished the wicked spirits of the Ethelhael Valley.

Molly goggled and gaped. And she looked down at her hands — they too seemed to be made of light. Where was she?

"We are not anywhere," said John Broome in a rich, full voice, answering her thought. "We are ... between places. You set me free."

Set him free? Molly shook her head. "How?"

"You gave me your voice," Broome said. "You heard me, and you let me pour my anguish out until it was spent. You listened to me."

"Course I listened to you," blurted Molly. "You were my dad's flipping hero."

The Silentman looked sad. He said, "I have not been called a hero for a long time. Let alone a flipping one."

Molly stared. "Dad always wondered — I always wondered — why you killed all those people."

The Silentman winced with pain. He closed his eyes, opened them. "The Mayor of Howlfair hated that I was popular. He hated that I spoke against injustice. He had a friend — a bishop of the church, but secretly a fraud, a demon-worshipper — and often times the mayor would pay this bishop to help solve his problems by performing spells and conjuring devils. It was the bishop's idea to frame me, to turn the people of Howlfair against me and have me executed. After I was hanged, the evil bishop performed a vile ritual. He used black magic to summon me as a phantom. He infused my spirit with a scream of damnation that I could never let out. He commanded me to roam blindly, setting my hands on the people of my town and infecting them with my scream. He turned me into the Silentman."

"But why did the bishop do this to you?"

"To make everyone hate me. To utterly ruin my reputation for all eternity. To take the credit for defeating me — because when enough people had died, the bishop conjured me here and locked me in this tomb and spread the story that he had trapped me in a snuffbox and thrown the box into the Six Bridges Stream. In reality, he kept me here, in case he ever needed to release me again to do his bidding. Evil people are seldom able to relinquish anything that gives them power. The stories remember me as an evil ghost, a figure of blame." He shook his head. "There is no weapon so vile as *blame*."

Molly didn't have time to reply. For suddenly someone was shaking her.

"Thank you," said the Silentman, fading. "I have one last task to complete, and then a hard and dangerous journey to make, but I hope to meet your father at the end of it."

Then everything went black. With gargantuan effort Molly prised open her eyes to see Carl hovering over her as she lay curled up like an ear on one of the stone steps.

A Little Help

MOLLY COUGHED, CHOKED ON A RAGGED breath. "The Silentman... What happened?"

"He's gone," said Carl. "You let his scream out of your mouth and nearly burst my eardrums, and then..."

Molly's throat burned. It hurt to breathe. "Then what?" she croaked.

"Then he vanished," said Carl. "Molly, you just defeated the Silentman."

Struggling to sit up, Molly rubbed her throat. "No," she rasped. "I think I just rescued him."

"OK, whatever," said Carl, shaking his head. "Question is, who's going to rescue *us*?"

Only seconds later, the trapdoor far above the children splintered, busted, and sprang open.

Molly's heart lurched.

"Furlock," she croaked. "He's been waiting."

Carl squinted angrily up at the light. "Run — or fight?"

Molly didn't have time to answer — for there, in the light at the top of the first flight of stairs, beyond the iron gates, a shadow appeared.

O ye gods — a ghoul!

A frazzled little ghoul! Way too small to be a ghoul, actually — but possibly an imp!

A meow echoed. The creature, Molly realized, was not a ghoul or an imp but her own pet cat, her companion throughout a thousand-and-one adventures, a scraggly thing with very few of his nine lives left.

"Gabriel!" Molly coughed.

She and Carl mounted the stairs and bundled through the trapdoor, and Molly scooped up the cat and looked up to see a man standing in the moonlit hall, holding a sword.

Montague Banderfrith.

"Luckily, Molly, your cat is quite the sniffer dog," wheezed Banderfrith, to Gabriel's consternation. "It led me straight here — after rescuing me from those ghouls who've been posing as journalists."

"How did you find out they're ghouls?" rasped Molly, her voice still raw. One of her old sneakers had disintegrated. She squatted down and pulled it from her foot, and began wrestling with the lace of the other.

"I've been doing some undercover investigations since I was, ahem, evicted from my home," said Banderfrith, "and I discovered that you'd got yourself into quite a pickle and might need some assistance." He returned his sword to its walking-stick sheath. "Usually I'd prefer to let people solve their own problems — but lately a friend has taught me that everyone can do with a little help from time to time."

Gabriel sniffed.

"Mr Wetherill's hunting for Benton Furlock in Loonchance Manor," said Carl. "But it's a trap. He's going to run into some ghouls and chase them, and —"

"...and he'll need my help," Banderfrith interrupted, his moustache twitching. "Follow me. That lily-livered milksop couldn't hunt a haggis, let alone kill a ghoul in cold blood. Trigger shy, that man."

"Mr Banderfrith," said Molly croakily, pulling off the other sneaker and following Banderfrith in her holey striped socks, "what did Mr Wetherill do to make you think he's a coward? Was it when you were both in the Guild of Asphodel?"

Banderfrith looked over his shoulder, alarmed. "How do you know about the Guild of Asphodel?"

"Because she's Molly Thompson," said Carl, bumbling after Molly, towards the mausoleum's great doorway. "She always finds out about everything."

Banderfrith sniffed, perhaps approvingly. "There was a time when Wetherill and I thought a monster was about to attack us. Wallace had his muskets, and I shouted at him to shoot the fiend as it sprang from a hedgerow — but Wallace froze. If it had been a monster, we would have been dead."

Molly chewed her lip. "But, um, was it really a monster?"

"It was a badger," said Banderfrith tetchily, heaving open the door to the mausoleum. "But that's not the point. The point is that I relied on the old fool to pull the trigger, and he didn't."

"This time he's going to pull the trigger," said Molly, following Banderfrith into the night. "He's been waiting for a chance to prove that he's not a coward. But this time he needs us to stop him."

Banderfrith paused in the moonlight. He eyed Molly warily. "Stop him?"

"We need to stop him from killing two humans who he thinks are ghouls," Molly said. Mr Banderfrith looked blank. She grabbed his elbow. "Let's go — I'll explain on the way to Loonchance Manor."

The Taste of Ghoulsbane

EVENING FANNED ITS CLOUDY PLUMAGE, opened its silvery eye — the moon — and fixed its glare upon a house that stood on a roundabout.

Loonchance Manor was wooden and crooked, and it leaned at an alarming angle, dipping towards the top of a neighbouring yew tree like a vampire sniffing the hair of a sleeping damsel.

Recently, Loonchance Manor had changed a bit. More than a bit.

Since Benton Furlock had vanished, the tourist board had taken back control of Loonchance Manor. Now it wore a big yellow banner:

* GRAND REOPENING THIS WINTER *

THE LOONCHANCE MANOR

FUN-AND-FRIGHTS FANTASIA

Join Gilbert the Ghoul and his grisly
gang for an educational tour of
Howlfair's WACKIEST attraction!

Gone was the large wooden sign that had previously advertized Benton Furlock's World-Famous Loonchance Manor Ghoul Tour, and which had described the place as a "blood-splattered murder mansion", wooing passers-by with mention of massacres and of ghouls eating children alive.

Scaffolding bound the exterior. Looking up, Molly saw that the roof was being rebuilt on the north side.

Also, it was hard not to notice that the outside of the house had been painted piglet pink and powder blue.

The cheery new look didn't fill Molly with much cheer as Gabriel led the group towards the round-about. The sight of the house, which wore a trailing hula skirt of blueish fog, had lost none of its power to make Molly's bones creep within her flesh. And not just because she'd nearly been killed in the crypts below it.

"No time for slack-limbed dallying," said Banderfrith as he drew alongside Molly and Carl at the gate to Loonchance Manor. "Follow me closely. Wetherill's so clumsy that he's bound to have left a trail of devastation for us to follow."

He began kicking the gate. Carl cleared his throat politely, reached down and opened the latch. Montague muttered thanks, then turned to eye Molly.

"Come on, girl. There's nothing to fear. If there are any *real* ghouls in there, they'll taste the silver blade of Ghoulsbane!" Mr Banderfrith whipped the gleaming sword from his walking stick, taking off a bit of Carl's floppy fringe. A cloud of hair rained gently to the ground.

Not feeling particularly reassured, and with a strange, growing sense that there was something important she was forgetting, Molly trotted after Mr Banderfrith and Carl, down the path towards Loonchance Manor. Hoping they weren't too late. Hoping they weren't heading into a trap.

Gilbert the Ghoul

MOLLY EXPECTED TO HEAR A SINISTER creak as the door opened, but the door swung smoothly on oiled hinges to reveal the hallway, freshly painted in orange. The last time she'd seen this room, it'd been dark and sinister and cobweb curtained, with model ghouls lurching waxy faced from the gloom. Now, the only familiar sight was the reception desk, next to which stood a large green Gilbert the Ghoul.

Gilbert the Ghoul did not look like a ghoul. At least, not like any ghoul Molly had nearly been devoured by. With his cheerful but careworn face and unhealthy colouring, Gilbert looked like a children's television character whose job was to communicate the importance of vitamins. He didn't even look like something a real ghoul might shape-shift into. He was...

A toy ghoul made of wool.

The lobby's previous ghouls, Molly remembered, had been looming waxwork things that looked as though they might come to life at any moment. Gilbert, conversely, looked like he'd unravel if you touched him. He grinned his sickly deathbed grin as the trio passed the reception desk. Molly found it difficult to pull her eyes away.

"This way," said Banderfrith, pointing his sword towards a narrow door. "Trust me — that cat of yours isn't the only one who knows how to track someone."

He flung open the door and some mops fell on him. Briefly he fought them, while Gabriel settled patiently near the door to the downstairs parlour and waited.

"I think Mr Wetherill might have gone, um, this way," said Molly, pointing to Gabriel.

"Yes, yes," coughed Banderfrith, reddening. "After entering the mop cupboard, the old coward no doubt proceeded into the parlour..."

The parlour had been painted tangerine and was gloomily lit by back-up lighting that came on as the group entered the room. Lanterns — electric, but designed to look like old-fashioned oil burners — hung from the walls. A CAUTION: PAINT sign had been kicked over, and a tin of paint had toppled sideways, projecting an orange oil slick across the floor.

Large colourful boot prints led to an archway.

"This is going to be easier than expected," said Banderfrith as Gabriel jumped over the paint puddle and proceeded through the archway into the gloomy corridor beyond.

"Are you OK?" Carl asked Molly bashfully. The last time they'd journeyed together through Loonchance Manor, Furlock had been dragging Molly by a rope wrapped around her head, and Carl had been helping him.

"Something's not right," said Molly.

"Don't worry," said Carl. "I'm not going to let anything happen to you." He slipped on some paint and righted himself. "Also, we have Ghoulsbane to protect us."

At the nearby stairway, where previously Molly had travelled down into the cellars, Gabriel now led the gang upwards.

Halfway up, his ears swivelled, and Molly thought she heard the sound of clattering far above them.

"He's in the attic."

"We need to hurry," said Carl.

She did not know — how could she have known? — that, back in reception, a woolly ghoul had opened his mouth in a grin to reveal a row of very real brown fangs, and had drifted eerily from his place next to the reception desk.

She did not know that the ghouls she'd trapped in Loonchance Manor that summer — all of them except the two that had been impersonating the Corcheses — had been hiding in plain sight all this time, disguised as the woolly toy ghouls installed to give the place a family-friendly feel for the grand reopening in the winter. The *real* toys — Gilbert and various silly knitted friends — had been disposed of.

In the parlour, the ghoul's shroud slid through the pool of paint, leaving a streak as he approached the archway leading to the stairs.

Glenda, Gavin, Gertrude

U P, UP. FLOOR BY FLOOR, FOLLOWING THE footprint trail.

All of the house's most grisly features were, apparently, in the process of being removed. The famous waxwork ghouls that had previously populated the rooms were gone, replaced by various knitted dolls — Glenda the Ghoul, Gavin the Ghoul, Gertrude the Ghoul — each more gormless than the last. The information boards recounting hideous histories had been taken down. But as Gabriel led the troupe up through the levels of the mansion, Molly realized that they were heading into parts of the building not yet touched by renovation. Here, horrors remained.

The noose with which Captain Emmet Pogson, a guest of the Loonchances', had hanged himself after a séance, still swung from the rafters of one circular chamber, moved by an unfelt breeze, or perhaps an unseen hand.

The masonry that had been pulled away from the south wall of the infamous Scarlet Room — in which an unfortunate dessert cook had been bricked up alive for making a mistake over a mere trifle — had not yet been replaced. Molly could see the cook's skeleton in the dark nook.

Magical symbols written in blood remained on the walls. And Molly saw, on the floorboards, magic circles used to protect sorcerers during the summoning of devils.

As the group ascended towards the attic — and towards the building's half-finished roof — the swells and booms of a storm grew louder. It was impossible to hear, over the weather, whether Wetherill was near.

Molly followed Carl and Mr Banderfrith, who in turn followed Gabriel, who followed the orange footprints. And one by one, a gang of Gilbert's hideous knitted friends — Glenda, Gavin, Gertrude — rose horribly from their perches, their glass eyes coming to life, their teeth elongating as they resumed something of their true forms — and followed Molly.

And at last, as Molly headed through an archway with a sign above it — **ATTIC — DANGER — ROOF UNDER RECONSTRUCTION** — and wobbled after

Carl up a very narrow wooden staircase, she heard Mr Wetherill's voice nearby, dimly but definitely.

"Halt, infernal fiends!"

They'd found him.

Mounting desperation livened Molly's limbs and she pushed past Carl, who wasn't coping well with the stairs.

Banderfrith, exhausted, had fallen behind. At the top of the stairs, through an archway, a corridor crowded with awful portraits stretched ahead, and Molly scooped up Gabriel and headed for the sound of Mr Wetherill's voice.

"Don't shoot them, Mr Wetherill!" she cried, tripping over her feet as she ran for the door to one of the attic rooms. "They're not ghouls!"

Gabriel under one arm, Carl following closely, Banderfrith still wheezing up the stairs, Molly wrenched open the door.

Farewell to Arms

THE ROOM WAS LIKE FOOTAGE FROM EVERY haunted-house film Molly had ever seen, spliced together. Large, lit eerily by gas lamps, the room was filled with furniture covered with dust sheets; a deep-voiced wind, entering freely through a moonlit gape in the roof overhead, inflated the dust sheets so that they threatened to rise like spectres. The sheer number of old portraits on the walls made Molly feel hemmed in by a dour-faced mob of the dead. Cobwebs hung in corners, from rafters, from the awful slanted grandfather clock in the corner.

There in the middle of the room, his muskets aimed at two hypnotized journalists, was Wallace Wetherill.

"Mr Wetherill, it's a trap! Put down the guns!" Wallace Wetherill spun, dropped a musket on his foot, scooped it up.

"She's right, Mr Wetherill," said Carl, tumbling

through the doorway. "Furlock's probably watching us from the next room."

Wetherill glanced at the Corcheses, then back at Molly.

"What if you're *all* ghouls?" he warbled, aiming one musket at Carl and the other at Molly, in whose grip Gabriel was squirming.

"We're not ghouls, Wallace," came a voice from the doorway — and in wheezed Mr Banderfrith, dragging his sword. "And neither are those two journalists. So listen to the children and *don't shoot.*"

"Bit of a turnaround, you telling me not to shoot, Banderfrith!" Wetherill warbled. "You kicked me out of the Guild of Asphodel for not shooting a badger, remember?"

"Back then you were right not to shoot, Wallace," Banderfrith said. "I was wrong. *Not shooting* is what makes you so valuable to the Guild of Asphodel, Wallace. You are a man of peace — that's why we need you. But if you shoot now, I swear I won't let you back into the Guild."

The hypnotized Corcheses watched dumbly.

"Let me back in? But you disbanded the Guild!"

"It's time we got the old gang together again," said Banderfrith. "Evil is afoot in Howlfair. But we can't start to fight it unless you put down your weapons."

341

Molly watched as Wetherill's huge hands quivered. They quivered so violently that she was afraid he'd accidentally pull the triggers. She looked at the Corcheses — how odd to see the *real* Corcheses, two hypnotized humans! — as they swayed, dazed, unseeing. Then she let out a long, relieved breath, jagged lumps of air pulsing from her chest, as Wallace Wetherill dropped to one knee and laid his muskets down.

At that moment the door behind Molly, and the door at the other end of the attic room, burst open and in flew the horrid woollen ghouls of Loonchance Manor, now a disgusting mixture of knitting and rotten grey flesh — and, with them, heavy moustache hanging, was Benton Furlock. Behind him were the two ghouls Molly had called Lucinda and Orson Corches, also transformed, eye sockets black, mouths hinged open and lower jaws missing, upper jaws studded with misshapen fangs.

Molly and her companions were surrounded.

Quite the Reunion

A S WETHERILL BENT PAINFULLY TO GRAB
his muskets, two of the ghouls flew at alarming
speed across the attic room and snatched them from
the floor.

"I confess I'm disappointed," Furlock said, his
bony white face every bit as ghoulish as those of his
infernal servants. "I was looking forward to seeing
the spineless Wallace Wetherill make up for ten years
of cowardice by shooting two innocent — or relatively
innocent — journalists."

The woollen ghouls cackled wetly. They sounded
to Molly like coffee percolators malfunctioning.

"But never mind. It is some consolation to have not
only gutless Wetherill, meddling Molly Thompson
and the orphan boy here at my mercy, but my old
friend Montague Banderfrith too! Montague, you
must be impressed with young Molly here — hell only

knows how she managed to escape the Silentman."

Banderfrith said nothing, but with a *swish* he raised Ghoulsbane high —

Before Molly could warn him, one of the woollen ghouls had glided behind him and plucked the sword from his hand.

Banderfrith cursed softly.

"Ah, this is quite the reunion!" cried Benton Furlock, raising his voice to compete with a sudden roar voiced by the storm that writhed above the mansion. "I almost wish we had time to share some stories of bygone days." The moonlight from the gape in the roof caught the hollows of his face and the diamond-shaped bald patch that crowned his cranium. "But we have very little time to spare, dear guests, and before the Silentman rises to fulfil the prophecy that Thompson and Grobman have triggered, I think I would like for my ghouls to eat you alive. On my command…"

He slid his left arm from his military jacket, and his mysterious crystal hand caught the moonlight.

"The Silentman isn't rising," Molly blurted. "He's at peace. He's gone. He won't be fulfilling your prophecy."

"Yeah!" said Carl. "Molly turned him *nice*."

For a moment Furlock looked discombobulated. Then he smirked.

"A prophecy is a prophecy," he said. "You cannot

cancel it. You cannot reshape it. And Howlfair's prophecies never fail to come true. Now, back to the matter of your devourment…"

Molly shook her head. Furlock was right. She'd said it herself, to Mr Wetherill, only days ago: *Howlfair's prophecies always come true — sooner or later.*

She'd rescued John Broome from his eternal madness. But she hadn't managed to rescue Howlfair from the prophecy.

Carl, by her side, stood with his fists ineffectually clenched, his legs wobbling. Wetherill had spread his hands out like a goalkeeper, as though hoping to intercept any ghouls attempting to attack his friends. Gabriel ceased wriggling and peered up at Molly quizzically — then followed her line of sight.

Reflected in the glass of the grandfather clock was a familiar face made of silver light.

The outline of a handbell.

She gasped.

"John Broome said he had one last thing to do," Molly whispered to Gabriel.

The cat meowed.

"I think so, too," Molly said. "He's going to fulfil the prophecy — but in his own way."

Slaves and Friends

FURLOCK'S CRYSTAL HAND REMAINED POISED as he searched to see what merited the look of wonder.

"Now we fight," growled Mr Banderfrith over the sound of the wind above the roof, though there was helplessness in his voice. "We fight with everything we have!"

He pulled off his toupée. Some of the ghouls giggled.

Wetherill checked his pockets and pulled out a potato peeler. Carl produced a bus pass and held it out like a switchblade. Gabriel rolled his eyes.

Molly looked up at the ghouls that surrounded her little troupe, and which were now returning fully to their original forms; their clothes turned to tattered shrouds decorated with stolen grave-jewellery; the foreheads shrunk away; the eyes bulged; the teeth turned brown and twisted. Their hair, straggly and dead, was whipped up by a new wind that tore slates and tarpaulin from the roof, letting the silver of the moon pour in. Furlock's crystal hand twitched, and one of the ghouls — Gavin — licked its teeth.

Banderfrith flung his oily wig at it —

Molly reached out and caught the wig.

"No," she said firmly. She looked back at the clock. The face was gone, and now it seemed a shape was forming in the corner of the room. "We don't need to fight. The Silentman wants us to see him do something flipping amazing."

"What are you talking about, brat?" Furlock snapped.

"He's going to find a different way to fulfil the prophecy. A better way."

The moonlight filled the attic now; the wind gave a roar; the white sheets over the furniture rose into the air like theatre tricks and vanished up into the night.

"The Silentman isn't out there in Howlfair, Furlock," Molly said, pointing to the window. "He's here. In Loonchance Manor. In this attic. Right now. And he won't be happy if you kill his friends."

Opening its mouth wide, the wind bit away half the roof and spat it into the sky; Furlock cringed and recoiled as beams from the roof fell. Wetherill cried out. Carl clung to Molly's arm. Banderfrith spun around, mouth open, as dust cascaded. Molly felt a thrill as she saw silver moonlight gathering in the corner of the room near the clock.

"His f-friends?" Furlock stammered as a wooden beam split and swung past him, breaking off and impaling a table. The wind shrieked along the walls. The spangles of silver moonlight began to knit together to compose a humanoid figure in the corner of the room. "What are you talking about, girl? The Silentman has no friends!"

"You wouldn't know about friendship, Furlock," Molly shouted, waving a hand. "You only know about slavery, don't you? These stupid ghouls are your slaves, and you're a slave of stupid Lady Orgella." It felt good to call Lady Orgella stupid. She thumped her chest with a fist, a gesture made more dramatic because her fist was gripping Banderfrith's wig. "I've got friends in high places." She pointed the wig at the corner of the room. "High places like this attic."

Furlock turned. The ghouls turned. Gilbert whimpered and pulled fretfully at a loose thread. Banderfrith gasped.

Wetherill shouted, "Jumping jeepers!"

Carl said, "Molly, what the heck's going on?"

"Like I said," shouted Molly, "the Silentman's here to fulfil his prophecy."

As Hellish As I

THE SILVER FIGURE, DAZZLING, ROSE TO FULL height — a town crier made of light, hefting a silver bell of stinging brightness.

Benton Furlock staggered to avoid a piece of scaffolding that the hurricane wind had escorted down into the attic. He fell sideways and flailed as the Silentman, almost too bright to look at, materialized.

"You — you're not the Silentman!" Furlock objected. "Your mouth... Your mouth... The plate over your mouth... It's gone! And your bell..." Furlock let out a sob. "In the books it is always pictured as streaming with hellfire!"

Then the phantom spoke, and the boom of Broome's voice shamed the storm.

"The bell is as it once was, when it was first blessed by the Order of Saint Fell, in the saint's secret tomb," he intoned. "It is once again a bell of banishing."

"But … the prophecy!" Furlock cried as, petrified, his ghouls flattened themselves against the attic walls. The shimmering phantom raised the piercingly bright bell, and a vortex of light spangles transfigured the chamber. "The prophecy says you will summon all those as hellish as you!"

John Broome looked at Molly. It was hard for her to look at him directly. But she thought she detected a smile.

"I will," said Broome. "But I am no longer hellish."

He rang the bell.

At first Molly heard nothing. Gabriel dropped from the cradle of her arms to the floor. Banderfrith's wig fell from her hand and landed on the cat. She realized then that her arms had gone dead, were hanging heavy, and that within every atom of the attic's atmosphere, a pure, high-pitched ring, almost too pure to bear, was singing. Her vision swam as the radiant phantom continued to ring the bell. Her friends were wobbling, jellified. The ghouls were screaming silently and clutching their skulls. The ghoulish Corcheses were melting.

The real Corcheses remained dazed, blinking, swaying.

"I summon light to contend with the fiends of this valley," boomed Broome. "And I who am no longer hellish call forth from hiding only those spirits as hellish as I."

The scream of the wind merged with the song of the bell, and the silver spangles of light that fizzled in the air welded together to form a blinding ocean of silver, and then the storm and the bell chime and the silver luminescence joined together, and with a suddenness so startling it made Molly fall gasping to her knees, reality returned and ran headlong into her.

The ghouls were gone; only streaks of silver, smoking gently, remained. The Silentman was gone. Half the roof had been ripped away, and moonlight pulsed. Molly looked around at Wetherill, Banderfrith, Carl, all gasping and checking that they were still alive she looked down at the glossy wig, disconcertingly still, beneath which Gabriel sat. She looked up to see Benton Furlock staggering at the other side of the attic, clinging to a chair. He spluttered, trying to speak, his eyes bloodshot, his hair on end.

In his one real hand he held one of Mr Wetherill's muskets.

He gave up trying to speak, pointed the musket at Molly and fired.

The weapon spluttered.

Then Molly saw a bolt of purple fire traverse the room and incinerate Banderfrith's wig.

"Gabriel!" she cried.

Fall of Gabriel

THEN MOLLY HEARD A LITTLE VOICE, A CATTY voice, up in the rafters above Benton Furlock's head.

She looked up. Furlock looked up.

Meow!

Gabriel was there. He had his claws bared; his fur was fuzzed and furious as he flung himself at Furlock's face. Benton Furlock lobbed the musket aside; it exploded in the corner of the room with a *woof* of frog-coloured fire, incinerating the grandfather clock and bringing down a triangle-shaped chunk of roof. Green smoke that smelled like mouthwash and melted flippers rolled across the attic and engulfed everyone therein.

Molly choked. She felt a hand grab hers. Now bodies were jostling her, protective hands grabbing her, pulling her towards the door as more of the roof fell and the smoke turned beige and began to smell of hairspray and boardrooms—

"*Gabriel!*"

— and she heard Banderfrith cough. "It's OK — I've got the little critter. I've got him…"

And down the corridor they ran, down the stairs they ran, through the horrible murder mansion they ran, and when at last they burst wheezing from the front door, all of them — Gabriel and Wetherill, Banderfrith and Carl, the hypnotized Corcheses — were alive and present, and Benton Furlock was nowhere to be seen.

"We lost him, damn it!" cried Banderfrith, raising a fist. He pulled up his sleeves and set his face towards Loonchance Manor. "I'm going back in."

"Let him go, Monty," wheezed Mr Wetherill, who'd bent over and put his hands on his knees. He straightened, clutching his hurt ribs. "His ghouls are gone. If Furlock's got any sort of brain, he'll stay away from Howlfair."

"But what about the prophecy, Mr Wetherill?" asked Molly. "Are the Dark Days going to come back straight away?"

Wetherill shook his head. The wound on his face had reopened; there was dried blood across one cheek, clogging a furry sideburn. "The prophecy never promised that the Dark Days would come back — just that the monster in the Crypt of the Blue Moon would summon those as hellish as he *till the Dark Days return*." He raised his eyes, adjusted his aviator specs. "But the monster was no longer hellish, and so those whom he summoned aren't hellish either. So I'm guessing that when the Dark Days do come back, the town of Howlfair will be ready. *Look*."

He pointed. Molly and Carl turned. Across the valley, little lights sparkled.

"What are they?" Carl asked.

"I think… I think they're good spirits," said Molly.

"Well, I never," said Mr Banderfrith, lifting Gabriel and placing him, absent-mindedly, on his bald head.

The wraiths twinkled, and vanished. One, up in the northern hills, seemed to Molly to linger a little longer before it winked and went. Molly wondered if it was her father.

Carl cleared his throat. "Quick question," he said. "What, um, are we going to do with these hypnotized journalists?"

Molly remembered that her mother was out searching for them. She sighed. "Let's start by taking them home."

Welcome to Howlfair

"HYPNOTIZED!" SAID GRAN, SWIGGING FROM a bottle of energy drink as Mr Banderfrith and Mr Wetherill arranged the catatonic journalists on Gran's bed. "We'd better sort them out before your mother gets back, Molly — she's combing the streets looking for them."

"But how do you de-hypnotize someone?" Carl asked.

"Wait here," said Gran, heading to the corridor. "There's a little trick I learned when I was a nurse..."

"Gran you've never been a nurse," called Molly, but Gran had gone.

Less than a minute later, Gran reappeared, heaving the fire extinguisher she'd hidden in a broom cupboard.

"Stand aside," she ordered, and before anyone could obey, Gran blasted the journalists with foam.

They leapt up, spluttering and dancing and gasping and covered in suds. The real Orson Corches bumped into a wall and fell over. The real Lucinda Corches began swearing loudly, covering her head with her hands.

"What's going on?" Orson coughed.

"Who are you?" Lucinda snapped at Molly. "And where the hell are we?"

Molly looked at Gran, at Carl, and then at the Corcheses. "You're in the Excelsior Guesthouse," she said. "Welcome to Howlfair."

The Old Gang

WHILE GRAN MADE SANDWICHES FOR THE Corcheses and assigned them a room to dry off in and arranged to take them to Howlfair Infirmary in the morning so they could receive treatment for their mysterious memory loss, Molly and the others sat in the lounge drinking hot chocolate and discussing the future.

"Whether or not we've rid ourselves of Benton Furlock," said Banderfrith, "I believe that the necessity has arisen for a certain league of monster-hunters to reconstitute itself."

Mr Wetherill scratched his head and looked at Molly. "What did he just say?"

"He's saying it's time to get the old gang back together," Molly said.

"The Guild of Asphodel," said Carl.

"If that traitor Furlock decides to show up again,

we'll be ready for him," Banderfrith said, smoothing his moustache. "I'll speak to Doris and the others in the morning, and we'll arrange a meeting."

Carl whispered to Molly, "I still can't believe our form teacher is a monster-hunter."

"Doris," said Wetherill, "is the deadliest monster-hunter of all."

Molly smiled down at Gabriel, who was curling around the table legs. Then she saw him look up. She followed his line of sight towards the doorway through which the lobby was visible. Moments later, Molly heard the sound of tyres on gravel.

"Furlock," hissed Banderfrith, lifting a butter knife from the table.

Footsteps crunched.

The front door opened. Then a figure appeared at the doorway to the lounge.

It was Molly's mother, looking fed up. She glowered at the assembled group.

"You will not believe," she snapped, "the night I've had."

Galactic Cats

THE NEXT MORNING, WHILE MOLLY HAD A lie-in and Gran escorted the Corcheses to Howlfair Infirmary, Montague Banderfrith tidied his room. Even though he'd stayed up late, he had been up extra early. He finished polishing in plenty of time to join Mr Kmiecik for coffee in the lounge.

Then he and Meech and Mrs Hellastroom and some of Mrs Hellastroom's friends set about redecorating the Excelsior.

At some point Montague and Wallace would have to have a long talk with Molly and her friends. Especially Molly. There were things that Molly needed to know. About her town, about the future. About her father, and how he once led the group of monster-hunters known as the Guild of Asphodel.

Maybe Molly should be told that Benton Furlock had also been a member of the Guild. Before he turned evil.

But first, the grizzled old men would be meeting with Doris de Ville and a couple of others to discuss the reforming of the Guild of Asphodel.

Sharon Thompson would be there too. She was going to be the Guild's secretary, dietician and fitness trainer.

Visitors

MOLLY SLEPT SO DEEPLY THAT NIGHT THAT she didn't hear Gabriel hissing and meowing. She didn't see the transparent lady, the ghostly image of Lady Orgella, leaning over her, death's head moths orbiting her head. She didn't hear the words the beautiful, nightmarish lady spoke.

"Well done, Molly. You are everything I'd dreamed you'd be."

Gabriel clawed at the immaterial vision of the demon as she reached to stroke Molly's hair with a hologram hand.

"Together, Molly Thompson, we will we make a new Hell on earth," the Mistress of Ghouls whispered.

A paw swiped through Orgella's insubstantial hair and eye patch. The demon smirked at the screeching cat.

"Oh, shut up, Gabriel," she said. "We both know you're no angel."

At last Gabriel's meowing woke Molly from a galactic dream. She'd been looking up from the earth at a dazzling nebula crowded with inhabitable planets, guarded by a belt of dark drifting clouds. And someone familiar was with her.

John Broome.

"I wanted to thank you," he said in a rich but somewhat sheepish voice. He looked towards the sparkling nebula. "I'm off to face the music. It's time to meet the people I killed. And to meet your father, I hope. It's a dangerous journey, but I have some protectors."

He gestured towards his feet. Molly looked down and saw a host of glowing creatures.

"Cats?" Molly blurted — and now she realized she was dreaming. "Flying space cats?"

"*Excelsior* cats," he said. "Generations of them." And at that moment a whine from Gabriel nudged Molly's face and startled her awake.

"Hey, Excelsior Space Cat," Molly murmured. "It's OK — everything's OK." The memory of last night came back to her — not the adventure in Kroglin Mausoleum and Loonchance Manor, but the hours spent sitting up with Mum, listening to her apologize for letting Molly shoulder the responsibility of rescuing the Excelsior. Mum had promised to send the Corcheses, when they awoke, to a different guesthouse — last night her car had broken down outside the Blowbridge Tavern, and she'd learned that it was actually a pretty nice place inside, and the owners were lovely.

"Your gran says the Corcheses are still behaving weirdly," Mum had said. "Acting like they don't know where they are, and saying they have to meet their tour guide and write a feature about Howlfair. As though this whole week never happened!"

"Journalists can be so weird," said Molly.

"So you don't mind them not staying here?"

"Course not," said Molly. "We don't need any scatterbrained journalists to make the guesthouse a success. Not when we have such excellent vegetarian cuisine."

"And they'll need a new tour guide, I suppose," said Mum. "If they decide to stay."

"Definitely," said Molly. "I'm sure Lowry's dad will be delighted to do it."

It was a clean-aired day. Even the crypts beneath Kroglin Mausoleum had a strange freshness about them. Dust motes danced in the empty crypt of John

Broome, changed partners, and giddily swam out of the chamber, past the sealed vault next door, the one with the tiny plaque — almost obscured by moss — that bore the name of an ancestor of Lowry Evans:

Here lies Ailsa Hickmott
Beloved half-sister of Alicia

Meanwhile, Montague Banderfrith, up a ladder, fixing the lights in the lobby while Mrs Hellastroom barked orders at him, gave Molly a wink as she headed to the front door. She smirked self-consciously. She opened the door to the Excelsior to find a small gang of friends outside: Lowry, Felicity and Carl. The day glowed blue behind them, stark and fresh.

Felicity was on a bike. "Your taxi, ma'am," she said, and Molly climbed on.

"Where shall we have the first meeting of the Junior Guild of Asphodel?" Lowry said, trying to trip Carl up as Felicity rode in slow slaloming curves, cutting back and forth behind the walkers.

"Kroglin Mausoleum?" said Felicity.

Molly gave an exaggerated shudder. "Never again," she said. "Not a chance."

"How about Cakes 'n' Shakes?" said Lowry. "I

fancy an extra thick Malted Madness with whipped cream."

It sounded good to Molly.

They headed towards town. Gabriel watched them from a high window, and then he raised his eyes and looked at the scant skirmishing clouds and the blue sheet of sky, and up to the pale vanishing stars. To space and ghosts and all the Excelsior cats beyond.

NICK TOMLINSON is a former English, Drama and Special Needs teacher, academic learning mentor, singing waiter and admin clerk. He has performed in a sell-out show at the Edinburgh Fringe, accidentally camped on a military target range in West Africa and managed to pass his karate black belt grading despite choking on his gum shield. A lifelong bookworm, Nick has been writing stories since he was five. His adult novel, *Saint Valentine*, was published by Transworld. Nick lives with his wife, Jayne, on the Welsh/English border, near Hay-on-Wye.